TORAC

GUARDS OF CLAN ROSS

ALSO BY HILDIE MCQUEEN

CHAPTER ONE

THE LOOK OF shock at the realization that they'd been mortally wounded was something a warrior never forgot. Fighting to the death was Torac Bratton's life, however, it didn't make witnessing a man's last breath any easier.

His opponent's eyes lost focus as the life ebbed out of him, the sword falling from his hand he stumbled backward. Dropping to his knees he crumpled from the severity of his wound until finally collapsing forward onto the muddy ground.

One last exhalation and then stillness.

The scene was etched in Torac's mind as he sunk down into the water. Torac kept his eyes open while holding his breath as if it were possible to erase the picture from his mind.

When his lungs protested, he remained just a bit longer before surfacing from the frigid water of the creek and inhaling loudly.

The soreness from days of riding and sleeping outdoors disappeared for a few moments as he stood in the chest-high water while scanning the bank. His clothes remained atop a rock, where he'd left them. Nearby his huge warhorse, Brutus, nibbled on green grasses, his tail swishing from side to side.

It was times like this that he felt the overwhelming loneliness of his life as a warrior. As of late, a stirring within had made him more reflective than usual. Perhaps it was the news that his half-sister, Cait, and her husband, Struan Ross, were expecting their second child. He was almost ten years older than Cait and had yet to sire a bairn.

That the last battle had left him so bothered was a sign that perhaps his time was up. When a warrior lost perspective, it could be deadly. There was a longing that Torac couldn't place.

Was it time for him to leave the laird's guard and begin a new life?

At the thought Torac groaned and dived back under the water. When he came back out this time, he walked toward the bank. It was time to mount and once again patrol the farm-lands ensuring all was right before returning to the guard post.

He'd asked to work alone and sort out things. The other leaders had not hesitated in agreeing as it was in everyone's best interest for him to be focused.

SINCE HE AND the other leaders had arrived in the southwest-ern corner of South Uist with a group of guardsmen, they'd battled against rebel villagers and encroachers who'd arrived by boat. But in the last few months, they'd mostly dealt with arguments between landowners.

The constables of the two villages they protected usually saw to the disagreements unless they got out of hand, at which point, Torac and his men were called to intervene.

At the sensation of being watched, Torac scanned the area using every skill he possessed as a seasoned warrior. He'd come to trust not only his instincts but those of Brutus. The warhorse lifted its head and sniffed the air. Then seeming not to sense any danger, trotted to the creek and began to drink.

Stark naked, Torac went to the rock where his clothes and sword were and grabbed his tunic. The entire time, he continued to scrutinize the surroundings without turning his head.

There was a slight movement behind a tree, a strand of hair had been caught in the branches unbeknownst to whoever hid. The silken red tresses could only belong to one person, and he concealed a smile.

He didn't wish her to go, so he turned back to his horse and stretched his arms over his head. Torac was especially proud of his backside, thick thighs, and broad back.

Then just to be sure she saw, he turned to look over his shoulder just in time to catch her ducking back behind the tree.

The lass was called Leana MacKern, according to a farmer he'd asked. The farmer had also insinuated that Leana was daft or had some sort of ailment that kept her from speaking clearly. He'd approached her once and she'd slapped him. She'd seemed terrified and timid, but not daft.

Once dressed, he strapped his sword to his back and stared at the tree. "I know ye are there Leana."

There was a bit of movement, but finally she peeked out, her eyes taking him in. Obviously noting he was now dressed.

"What is it?" Torac said. "Do ye require help?"

She came from behind the tree, her eyes downcast, and nodded. "Aye. My father is injured." Her voice was melodic and soft, the strong lilt making it seem as if she sang rather than spoke.

"What happened?"

A tear trailed down her right cheek. "I dinnae know exactly. His leg is lame."

"Brutus," Torac called to his steed. His ears perked, but other than that, the horse ignored him.

He stalked to the animal and mounted, then after guiding the huge warhorse over to Leana he held down a hand. "Grab my hand with both of yers," he instructed.

After a slight hesitation, she did as told, and he pulled her up to sit sideways in front of him. By her fast breathing he could tell she was not at all comfortable with the proximity of their bodies.

"Where is yer home?" He had an idea of the area but wasn't sure which farm her father owned. She pointed in the direction of her home, and they headed off.

Perhaps because the woman between his arms was in distress, Torac could not help but feel protective over her. There was a fragility about her that brought out that side of him. Although by the hard slap, months earlier, she was not exactly a fragile creature.

"Why did ye not go to the village to seek help?" he asked her.

Leana let out a long sigh. "I was on my way there when I saw ye. I thought perhaps it would be faster if ye took my father there. I cannot help him to the wagon alone."

He noted she'd not ridden to the village, but he understood. On foot running through the woods was a much shorter distance than going all the way around with a horse and cart.

They arrived at a cottage beside fields of what looked to be wheat. There were a few animals in pens. Although it was a small farm Torac conceded that it no doubt provided for all their needs.

Men who farmed and had livestock were hard workers who were much appreciated by the laird. They kept people fed and were not a burden on others.

Without his assistance, Leana slid from the horse and hurried into the house. Torac dismounted and then followed her inside.

Ducking to enter through the front door, at once he saw a man lying on a blanket. His left leg had been tied to a splint and he was asleep.

"What happened?" Torac asked Leana kneeling next to the man lying on the floor. The man opened his eyes at the sound of Torac's voice, so he redirected his question to him, "Ye broke yer leg?"

"Aye," the injured man replied. "Kicked by a cow of all things." He smiled at his fretting daughter. "'Tis nothing to worry too much about Leana. There was no need to bother someone."

"I am called Torac. I agree there is little that can be done, other than find ye a more comfortable place to lay." He looked to Leana, who averted her gaze.

Her father gave Torac an unreadable look. "Can ye bring my bed in here? I can see about things from in this room without too much worry."

Together, Torac and Leana shifted the furniture already in the room to one side and then moved the man's bed into the space. Once she put a blanket atop, Torac lifted the man carefully and placed him on it.

It was obvious by the grunts that the man was in a great deal of pain.

Leana hurried to the kitchen and returned with a cup of something and put it in her father's hands. "Herbs to help with the pain."

"I am called Eli," the man said to Torac. "Thank ye."

"Is there someone nearby who can come and help with the farm?" He motioned to the side where the fields were. "If not, I can bring my men to help with the harvest. It seems to be almost time."

The farmer's face brightened. "That is my biggest concern. The sale of the wheat feeds us through the winter and pays my taxes to the laird."

When Torac turned to speak to Leana, she was gone.

"The lass is not comfortable around people. Has been shy since she was a bairn. Thank ye for yer offer of help." The man closed his eyes and let out a long breath. "If ye dinnae mind, I will rest for a wee bit."

It was late afternoon, which meant it would be dark by the time he arrived back at the guardhouse. However, Torac was determined not to spend another night outdoors.

He searched around the house for Leana, but it seemed the lass had left. When the sound of huffing caught his attention, he found Leana pushing a wheelbarrow with a sickle and other items sticking out of it at all angles.

"Ye do not have to do the work. My men and I will be here to help in a pair of days. Look after yer father."

She lowered the wheelbarrow, her gaze moving past him, then to the side, and finally to the ground. "Ye have done enough for us. No need to return. Father and I can do for ourselves."

"Does yer father not seek help during harvest?" Torac had

a hard time believing the older man and the wee lass could handle all the work alone.

"He goes to the village and hires some help," she finally replied. "There is no need for yer men to be put out."

"What do ye plan to do with all of that?" He pointed to the items in the wheelbarrow.

"Nothing," she replied much too quickly. "I am just sorting them out."

There was little he could do other than let the lie go. "Like I said, we will return two days hence."

"How delightful that strong men come to assist." A woman appeared from the side of the house. Hips swaying and gaze locked on his, the woman approached without sparing Leana a glance. "Has something occurred that ye are here warrior?"

Torac nodded. "Aye, Eli has broken his leg. My men and I will return to assist with the harvest."

The woman's eyebrow lifted, and she finally looked to Leana. "Interesting."

Her eyes lifted to him. "I am called Willa and live on the farm just beyond the fields. My brother once lived here." She motioned to Leana's house.

At her words, Leana hurried past them to the house, the sound of the door slamming behind her.

"What happened to yer brother?" Torac asked.

"He disappeared," Willa replied looking toward the cottage. "And they have something to do with it. I am sure."

Instead of asking anymore about the situation, he decided it was best to be on his way. "I must return to the guard post."

When he started to take a step, Willa's hands wrapped around his bicep. "Would ye like to go for a walk? There is little to do here, and I would be grateful for the company."

From the way she leaned into him, Torac was well aware of what she was offering and despite his better judgment, he considered it.

There was movement at the window, probably Leana watching them.

"Ye can walk with me to get my steed, but I really must go."

Willa pouted. "When ye return, I will ensure ye and yer men have food and drink. My brother makes a very good ale."

"It will be appreciated," Torac said as they reached the corral where Brutus pawed the ground and swung his huge head. The animal was trying to impress the mare, who was oblivious.

It took a few moments to disentangle himself from the eager Willa and he mounted, urging Brutus to a gallop in hopes of arriving at the guardhouse before too late.

As he rode away, he considered what an interesting day it had come to be. He'd planned to swim, patrol, perhaps stop at a tavern before heading home. Instead he'd been approached by two women with very different reasons. And he'd done a good deed, helping Eli from laying on the floor.

Questions swam around in his head. Why had Leana not gone to any of her neighbors for help?

Who was Willa's brother and why did she blame Leana for his disappearance?

Lastly, why did Leana try to refuse help from him and his men?

He shrugged off the questions. Whatever happened between the people was none of his concern unless they were called to intervene.

Should he have taken Willa up on her offer? It had been many months since he'd lain with a woman. No one would know if they'd snuck off into the woods. Except for Leana, who would have known he was still there because of Brutus' presence in the corral.

The weather was warm, and it was obvious his steed enjoyed the run across the open space. As they rode past the creek, Torac turned to it.

How much of him had Leana actually seen?

CHAPTER TWO

"**H**AS HE GONE?" Leana's father asked from his bed. From the window, she could still make out Torac as he rode away, his horse at a fast canter. "Aye, he just did. After talking with Willa."

Her father chuckled. "The lass can smell a man and appear with little notice."

"It is not our concern, but I do not like her about. She has a vile tongue." Leana turned to face her father. "Ye know as well as I do, she blames us for Gawyn's disappearance."

"Let it go Leana. There is naught to be done about it. She has a right to be angry. Not knowing what happened to her brother."

A shiver went down her spine at recalling the man who'd brought nothing good to their home. If anyone deserved to be angry and bitter, it was her. He came into her life, dashed every dream, and then left leaving her afraid of her own shadow.

Although she'd always been shy, now terror and distrust of men made it almost impossible to be around people. It was as if a deep panic set in that barely allowed her to think.

In the back of her mind, she pictured Gawyn catching her speaking to a man and accusing her of horrible things. He'd done that, had berated her, and acted as if she had little sense.

Although they'd not married, he'd claimed her as his wife, and they'd been living together there at her father's farm for almost a year. One morning, Gawyn left without a word. He'd packed his clothes, taken all their money, and left.

Almost a year had passed and every day she felt his presence. Sensed him watching. It was doubtful, of course. In reality, he'd probably gone and left the isle to seek a new life elsewhere.

She prayed he never returned.

"I will go check on the animals. Do ye require anything?" At no reply, she turned to see that her father had fallen back asleep.

Carrying a basket of chopped apples, Leana walked out to find the goats jumping up and down, excited at the prospect of the treat. Her lips curved at their antics. "Aye, I have apples for ye."

She held out the cut-up pieces, ensuring each of their six goats got a fair amount. Then she went to where the mare was keeping an eager eye on her and fed her whole apples.

Once that was done, she returned to the kitchen door and lifted a bucket filled with leftovers from their meals, some bread chunks, and more apple pieces.

The pigs were not as excited to see her, but both lifted their heads to watch her approach and upon deeming the food she placed in their trencher worthy, walked over to it, snorting the entire time.

The cows fed on hay that had been placed out for them by her father earlier in the day, prior to milking the cow that had kicked him.

She went to the corral where the offending animal grazed,

seeming not at all aware of what it had done. "Lout," Leana said to it. The cow lifted its head and gave her a lazy stare.

The days were getting longer, and she looked about the grounds making mental notes of what all had to be done before she went to bed.

Since the weather was nice, their mare would remain outside. The pigs and goats would be fine in their pens.

With a long breath, she retrieved a pail of grain and threw it out for the chickens. The birds hurried about eating and making so much noise, Leana laughed.

Once that was completed, she walked to the back of the house and sat down. The farm was small by most standards, but she and her father fared well. Never hungry and with the sale of the wheat, they had coin for most necessities.

Every day there was much to do. Animals to be fed. Garden to be tended. Thankfully, for a while now, a pair of lads, from a farm across the way, came weekly to chop wood for the stove and hearth.

It was a life Leana did not care to leave. Although at times she wished for friends and to be invited to gatherings, the fact she was so petrified at the thought meant she would never go.

A picture of Torac bathing at the creek suddenly popped into her mind and made her heart race. She placed a hand over her chest. He had been bereft of clothing and despite her urgency to go to the village to see about someone to help with her father, she'd stopped and watched him.

Never in her life had she seen a man built like him. It was as if he'd been bred for war. Every part of his body thick and muscular. Even the wide expanse of his back had been breathtaking.

When he'd turned and stretched, she'd drunk in the sight, her mouth going dry. She'd not dared to look down from his chest when he'd faced her, as she knew it would have been wrong. However, she'd caught a glance of the way his flat stomach was rippled, as if he'd been sculpted by an artist.

She'd barely breathed when riding to her home. Leana was ashamed to admit wishing the ride had taken longer, as she'd enjoyed every moment of sitting against him, his strong arms around her.

Her face was hot, and she fanned with both hands. There was a stirring in a place she'd rather not think about. How could it be that despite not trusting or caring for men, with Torac, so many emotions had surfaced that day.

Interest. Arousal. Even jealousy when Willa had hung on to his arm.

"Leana," her father called from inside. "Could ye help me for a moment?"

She stood and took one last look around. "Aye, Father."

MARKET DAY AT Welland was always a busy time. People traveled from many miles, to sell or purchase all kinds of wares.

People called out what they sold, claiming to have the best, as people walked by. Every stall was stocked with offerings of pots, baskets, linens, and foodstuff.

Constable Athol made his way past the stalls, intent on finding a quiet place to sit and enjoy a cup of ale whilst his wife meandered in the square with his youngest daughter in tow.

He'd almost made it to the tavern when Willa Brown blocked his way. "Ye are not even trying to find him are ye?" she said not having to clarify who she spoke about.

"Have ye gone to the MacKern farm and spoken to them at all?" She put her hands on her hips as if to block him from going any further. "Ye know something happened to my brother."

Athol met the young woman's gaze. "Ye should accept that yer brother left. He spoke about it at the tavern just before. Said he did not wish to continue to live here."

"He never said that to us. To Da or Mother. He would have never left without telling us."

Perhaps Willa had a point. But there was little chance of anything bad happening to Gawyn.

Athol let out a breath. "I went to the MacKern's farm and did a search. He took his clothes and their money. Eli was beside himself unsure how they'd survive the winter without coin to pay for things."

The young woman's face twisted with anger. "They lied." She leaned forward. "Ye do not believe me when I tell ye, something horrible happened to my brother. When the truth comes out, I will ensure everyone knows how little ye did."

With that, she rounded him and stormed away.

"What happens?" Helene, his wife walked up. "Is she still going on about that no-good brother of hers?"

"Whether he was a bad person or not, she has every right to be worried. However, I cannot find anything to prove other than he left on his own. The man should have said something to his family."

Helene followed Willa's progress. "Aye, he should have. I expected he would have."

The words were like cold water spilled over him.

After searching the village square and not finding either Eli or Leana about, Athol went to his house and hitched his horse to a cart. Then he rode out of the village. Perhaps he could ask more questions. Often after some time has passed, emotions lessened, and memories become clearer.

Leana opened the door, her gaze meeting his for a split second before she looked down. "Ye wish to speak to father? He broke his leg and is asleep at the moment."

The young woman was a beauty. There was a serenity about her that made one take pause. With vibrant red hair and a pretty face, she reminded Athol of the faes in the stories his mother told when he was a child.

"I can speak to ye a bit while I wait for him to waken."

The lass moved back to allow him into the house. Then upon him sitting at the table, she poured a cup of cider and placed it before him.

It was obvious she was unsettled, which he'd come to expect. Leana had always been shy and nervous.

"Willa approached met at the village square to ask again about Gawyn's disappearance," he started, noting that Leana swallowed visibly. "She claims he would have never left without speaking to them."

"I do not know what he would or would not do," Leana replied softly. "He was always so... angry."

Athol motioned to a chair. "Please sit, Leana. I am not here to make any accusations, but to find out what I can so I can answer his family's questions."

"Almost a year," Leana said as she lowered to a chair. "He has been gone for a long time."

"Can ye remember if he said anything about where he would go if he ever left Uist?"

Leana shook her head. "No. I do not think so."

It was well known that Gawyn mistreated Leana. She'd often accompanied him to the village, sitting silently on the bench next to him as they rode in. More times than not, she'd have visible bruises.

In truth, Athol hoped the man would never return. The poor lass did not deserve such mistreatment.

"Constable," Eli called from the bed. "Nice of ye to stop by. Be with care, I may give ye work to do."

He stood and walked over to where the farmer lay, his leg splinted. "What happened?"

While the farmer explained what happened, Athol took in the tidy space. There was no doubt that Leana was a good woman. The house was well kept, her father taken care of.

When Athol moved to sit next to where Eli was, Leana made the excuse of going to check on the livestock.

"What will ye do about the harvest? Should I see about men to help ye?" Athol asked.

"Nay," Eli replied. "A Ross warrior was here. Leana ran into him when she was going to seek help for me. He assured me that several of them will be coming in the next two days to do the work. I will not have to pay for it." Eli gave him a knowing look.

"A blessin' since we barely made it after Gawyn took off with all our coin."

Using the opportunity, Athol remarked. "Have ye not

heard from him then?"

"No! And if he dared to return, I will beat him away meself," Eli said with feeling. "He is not worth the dirt on my daughter's shoes."

"I agree, he was not kind to her at all."

They sat in silence for a bit before Athol broached the subject again. "Willa claims ye and Leana know where he went. She implies that something could have happened to him."

"Aye 'tis possible something happened," Eli agreed. "He took off in a hurry and without a proper plan. I suspect he left the isle. 'Tis nothing to do with us anymore. I am glad to see the back of him."

WHEN LEANA RETURNED inside, Athol was gone, and she let out a sigh of relief.

"Gawyn brings grief even after he leaves. I wish Willa would stop blaming us for his leaving. I did not expect it, but I am glad for it. I am afraid of him returning."

"He will not," her father said, his face stoic. "That man will never return here."

Leana went to her father and kissed his forehead. "Do not fret Da. Ye need to rest and get better. We have to get ye up into a chair when the men come to harvest, so ye can yell out orders."

The thought of it made her father laugh and Leana was glad to lighten the mood.

"I best get supper going." She went to the kitchen, her neck and shoulders tight from thinking about the constable's visit. Willa had a poisonous tongue and no good would come of her accusations. Hopefully people did not believe her.

Most knew Gawyn as a mean man who was constantly picking fights and unkind to people. Surely she and her father were not the only ones glad that he'd left.

CHAPTER THREE

I T WAS EARLY, the mist in the trees had not quite lifted as Torac made his way from the smaller post house to where the aroma of roasting meat lured him.

Auley, the camp cook, and the young lad who helped him were busy spooning porridge and a side of crisp meat into the bowls of warriors who'd lined up. A man, who'd come to live there with his wife and daughter, helped by passing out bread and cups of warmed cider.

His stomach growled in anticipation, but he waited patiently for his turn. Just then Struan, the archers' leader walked up. "I wonder if Erik misses times like this. The fresh outdoors and smell of good cooking."

"Waking up in a warm bed with a woman beats this," Torac replied with a shrug. "I would make the trade."

"Aye, but there is little chance of ye ever finding a willing one," Struan said chuckling. "Yer disposition runs them off."

He was well aware of his serious nature, however, he'd not lacked for a woman's company whenever he needed it.

Instead of replying, he looked across the way to where the man's wife and daughter were cooking.

"Have we ensured the men do not bother the lass?"

Struan followed his line of sight. "Aye. The father is very protective. He ensures she is rarely alone."

"So ye have been watching?" Torac remarked.

Struan shrugged. "A bit."

Over the meal, Torac told Struan about his plans to take men to assist the farmer with the broken leg.

"It will help foster confidence and trust when they see we are willing to help."

"Help with what?" Erik walked up and sat down. His hair was disheveled and there were bags under his eyes.

"What happened to ye?" Struan asked.

"No sleep. The bairn cried all night." Erik yawned widely. "What were ye talking about?"

"Torac wants to take men to help a farmer with his harvest. Broken leg. A cow kicked 'im." Struan took a big piece of meat and chewed it.

"Since the farmer usually hires from the nearby village, would we be taking work from local men who expect to do it? We can go to the village and let them know the farmer will pay for work," Erik explained.

"He told me to have no coin. Just a few men for a sennight, we can spare the time right now."

He continued to eat in silence while Erik and Struan considered his proposal. He didn't begrudge them. In their place, he would be considering whether or not doing farm work would take men away from more important duties.

"We can ask for volunteers and if what ye say is true, that the neighboring families are willing to feed them, then aye." Erik shrugged. "We are not so busy and perhaps the men need a distraction."

"We should still hire a couple of men from the village, or nearby farms, to ensure there are no grudges about it," Torac added.

"There is the matter of the men who've been stealing from families near Aldress," Erik stated, referring to the village near the farm they'd be going to. "This may be a good opportunity to catch them in the act."

The attacks on farmers had occurred infrequently over the last months, which made it hard to catch whoever was responsible.

They discussed the money that was sent regularly by the laird to pay for food and other necessities, as well as the warrior's wages and decided on an amount. A shilling a day would be paid to the men from the village to finish the work.

They waited until the guardsmen finished eating and had formed up for the morning's orders. It was easy to find volunteers. The men were indeed ready for a break from the monotony. Torac expected that the opportunity to be around women from the village was an added incentive.

They'd leave the next day and work at the MacKern farm for a sennight. Whatever wasn't done could be finished by the village men.

It was later in the afternoon that Torac rode out to meet the men who were to return from their patrol.

Brutus seemed glad to be out of the stables, although they'd been out riding for several days. The beast galloped and then slowed upon men appearing.

Torac held up his hand in greeting and the warriors rode to him and stopped.

One of them was Balgair, looked annoyed. "The worse thing we ran across today was a boar defending her young. There are no reports of anything from farmers."

Other than the infrequent robberies, during the past months, the lack of danger had given them the opportunity to get to know the people in the neighboring villages. There was little to worry about, except for being on guard for anyone coming from the sea.

Balgair, who was from the Isle of Skye, was restless and Torac understood, especially since there were rumors of battling between clans there.

"Several men are going with me to help harvest wheat and keep an eye out for the robbers. Do any of ye wish to go?" Torac didn't direct the question directly at Balgair. The muscular man was many things, but he definitely did not seem to know the first thing about farming.

"I will come with ye," replied Balgair. Torac and the men who accompanied Balgair all stared at him.

Balgair shrugged. "Why is that so shocking? I grew up on a farm."

"Very well, if ye wish, I could use ye in case the men who are causing trouble show up."

Balgair and his men rode toward the camp and Torac guided Brutus westward. It would be an hour or two to reach the shore. Once there he'd take a few moments to take in the salty air and consider the plans for the following few days.

As he expected, the salty air and sound of the waves lapping on the shoreline had the desired effect. Torac immediately relaxed.

He considered Willa's comments about her missing brother. The idea of a man disappearing was troubling. He had to find out what happened to Gawyn. It was not uncommon for a man to leave everything behind and start anew somewhere else. However, according to the sister, he had a good relationship with them and was planning to attend a family gathering. There did not seem to be a reason for him to suddenly leave.

Upon returning to see Eli, he would ask more questions. At the thought of the man with the broken leg, his thoughts went to Leana.

The quiet beauty was timid. More than that, it was as if she was terrified of men. She had the look in her eyes of a woman who had been mistreated and had lived in fear for her life.

Someone had affected the way Leana felt around men. Was it possible it was the same man who was missing?

Her father did not seem to notice that Leana gave Torac a wide berth while he'd been there, nor did the man act surprised when she walked out without a word. Perhaps he was used to her ways and had stopped noticing such things. Torac on the other hand was intrigued enough to take note of everything she said and did.

The sky turned into shades of vibrant colors, streams of light shooting up from the horizon as the sun began its descent. It was hard not to admire the view as Torac hesitated for a moment, before heading to get Brutus and return to camp.

WHEN THE MACKERN farm came into view, Torac slowed his steed and looked around the area. There were farmlands as far as the eye could see. In between fields needing to be harvested soon, cottages and barns blotted the view.

Horses grazed in corrals. Sheep did the same on the steep

hills. Every so often a cart and horse came into view either heading to or from the village.

It was a peaceful place, Torac considered. Families there and were close enough to others that they could give aid or receive it when required.

"Every shutter is closed," Balgair stated, looking at the MacKern's house. "Do ye think they've gone?"

Indeed the house did have an unwelcoming first impression. Unlike the time before when he'd been there, even the chickens were out of sight.

"Let us find out." He rode to the front of the house. When no one looked out, he guided the men to the back. Once there, they put their horses in a corral and went to the large barn to survey what tools there were.

It was then that Torac saw Eli. The man sat on a chair, his broken leg propped up. He waved him over a smile on his face.

"I am so very glad to see ye. That stubborn lass of mine is attempting to begin harvesting." He looked to the field where no one was visible.

"Where is she now?"

Eli frowned. "Probably inside the barn."

At that moment, Leana appeared. She hurried from the barn and straight to where Torac and her father stood. Her face turned a bright red and her chest lifted and lowered, with harsh breaths at being startled by the warriors.

"As ye knew, I promised to return with help." Torac ensured to keep his voice even. Although there was no reason to be afraid, she certainly seemed to have an unreasonable fear of men.

"Aye," she finally replied breathlessly. "It is that I did nae hear ye arrive."

"How could ye not have heard all the ruckus with the horses and such?" Her father admonished with a good-natured shake of his head. "'Tis that yer head is always in the clouds."

At her father's words, Leana's cheeks turned even a brighter pink. "I will show ye where the tools are."

"No need," Torac replied noting that his men emerged with various sickles and such.

While Leana stood frozen, seeming uncertain what to do, her father motioned to the fields with his right hand, pointing at a specific area. "The wheat from there to the road is ready for harvest. Should nae take more than a pair of days."

Torac walked to the edge of the house to survey the size of the area. In his estimation, with inexperienced men, it would take at least double the time.

"We will do what we can for a sennight. At that time, men from the village will be hired to take our place."

Eli looked dejected. "I cannot afford to pay them. I have no coin left. It was stolen…"

"Father," Leana interrupted. "Perhaps, we can offer to pay them once the wheat is sold."

"The laird will pay five men to work for a sennight," Torac informed them. "If all the work is not completed in that time, then ye can work out how to have it done."

With a wide grin, Eli nodded enthusiastically. "All should be completed by then. I have no doubt. I will travel to thank the laird in person once my leg heals."

"There is no need," Torac assured him. He kept to himself that the laird was not aware they were to pay men out of the money sent for the camp.

They began working right away, the warriors working with tools unfamiliar to them. Within moments, they followed Balgair's instructions and moved with more assurance.

"The wheat that is felled must be bundled and tied together," Leana said walking up to stand beside Torac.

Somewhat surprised at her coming close, Torac didn't look at her directly. "The warrior called Balgair grew up on a farm. He will ensure all is done well."

Taking advantage of the situation, he decided to bridge the subject of the missing man. "The woman Willa is adamant in that ye know where her brother Gawyn is."

Leana visibly tensed but remained silent.

"On our way here, we rode through Welland and were told by the constable there that Willa spoke to him asking that ye and yer father be questioned again. Why is she so insistent?"

For a long moment Leana stared into the distance, her gaze unfocused. Just as he was about to speak again and repeat the question, she looked at him.

"I pray every day that Gawyn never returns. Neither Da nor I had anything to do with his leaving. But I am glad that he did."

There was something she wasn't saying. Torac could feel it in his bones. "Why does Willa think ye did?"

Her shoulders lifted and lowered. "Because she knows I wanted him to leave." Her gaze fell to the ground. "It is hard for me to form the right words, to explain that if Gawyn left, it was because he wished to. No one can force him to do something."

It was evident that the subject was upsetting for Leana, so he let it drop.

"Who are ye hiring to help?" Leana asked, her gaze moving to meet his before darting away.

"I do not know. We will find workers."

"Please allow Father to do it." She turned to where her father leaned forward in his chair in order to see what the men were doing. By his expression, he found their efforts lacking.

"Father," Leana said walking toward him. "Ye will fall from the chair if ye keep leaning so far."

"I cannot see all of them. I must move out further." The man struggled, but he managed to get up from the chair to stand on his unbroken leg. He winced visibly as he waited for Torac to move the two chairs, one for his leg.

Once he was settled, Torac spoke. "Are there specific men that will come to help ye?"

The farmer nodded. "Aye, I will give ye their names. Two of the lads from across the way, the Mackinnon's, they will help."

"I best go and help," Torac said. Before he could walk, Leana touched his forearm.

It was but a light press of her fingers on his skin, but it may as well have been a torch by the way it affected him.

She met his gaze. "Thank ye. We would have been devastated watching our fields wither without the ability to harvest but a bit of it myself."

For a moment neither of them moved, their gazes locked. It was as if even the air stilled in anticipation of what was to be said next.

"It is what we are here to do. To help with things..." Torac let the sentence trail. Just as he was to speak again Leana dropped her hand and hurried away. It was then he noticed that Balgair had neared.

His gaze followed after Leana. "I was going to ask how far out we should go. We need to set a line."

Unsure what he meant, Torac motioned to the farmer. "Let us ask Eli."

Several people arrived late in the day and despite the fact Leana kept her distance from people, it seemed Eli was well-liked.

The food was simple but delicious. The men ate their fill before returning to work for a few more hours.

Willa was noticeably absent even though she'd assured him she'd be there, which made Torac wonder what the woman was up to.

By the end of the day, Eli had gone inside to rest as he'd finally agreed to take something for the pain. Unlike him, Leana kept busy. She fed the animals, worked in the garden, and then helped bundle the wheat. Working efficiently while keeping as far away from others as possible.

Despite it being hard work, Torac reasoned that he and his men would not have sore arms or backs even. The motion of cutting down the wheat stalks was like that of sword practice.

One warrior even went so far as to use his sword to cut down wheat, grunting loudly, pretending to down a foe. The others laughed at his antics until Balgair pointed out that he might be dulling his blade.

By the end of the day, they all settled around a fire, a short distance away from the house. They'd taken water from the well to wash off the sweat of the day and then eaten a simple last meal of bread and cheese that had been brought out by Leana.

"She is quite strange," Balgair said looking up at the sky. "Bonnie, but strange."

Torac couldn't help but chuckle. "Aye, very timid."

"Not with ye," the warrior said.

"It was I who helped when her father first broke his leg. I think she trusts me."

The night sounds coming from the nearby forest was lulling, making it easy to relax after a hard day's work. However, Torac couldn't stop thinking of the feel of Leana's hand on his arm. Why had it affected him so?

CHAPTER FOUR

O NCE ARRIVING IN Welland, Leana hurried to the market, her gaze downward to avoid having to speak to anyone. It was rare that she went to the village alone. Usually her father was with her and acted like a shield protecting her from having to approach too many people.

Although she'd always been timid, it was the trauma of her mother's death that had changed her completely.

IT WAS A dreary day when Leana was about twelve, she and her mother were returning from the village.

"I think men are following us. Cover up," her mother had urged Leana while looking over her shoulder. "No matter what, do not do anything. Remain still."

Just then the men on horseback caught up to them. "Yer much too bonnie to be left to ride alone," one of the men had called out.

"Leave us be," her mother replied.

The men's laughter had sent shivers down Leana's spine and despite her mother's directions, she'd peered out from the blanket over her head to get a glimpse of the men. They looked as if they'd been on the road for far too long, their clothes dirty, beards and hair untrimmed.

Leana ducked back under the blanket and leaned on her

mother.

"Stop and talk to us, we mean ye no harm." The man attempted at a kind tone without success.

"My husband awaits us ahead." This time her mother's voice was shaky.

Their cart came to a stop when one of the men pulled at the horse's reins. The gentle mare put up no resistance making Leana wish they'd a large strong horse instead.

Leana wasn't sure what happened other than her mother pushing her onto the floor of the cart and whispering. "Stay still darling."

Moments later one of the men approached, his voice hard. "Just a chat is all we wish for."

"Go away." Her mother screamed. "Please leave us alone."

The man grabbed her mother's arm yanking her forward. There was a scream followed by the sound of struggles. Then suddenly silence.

"Ye knocked her out," one man said. Leana peered out from under the blanket to note that her mother didn't stir.

The man with the gruff voice spoke next. "Her head hit a rock. I had nothing to do with it."

"Ye will hang for it."

Just then they looked up and must have seen someone coming because they mounted and race away.

Leana scrambled from the wagon, hurrying to her mother's unmoving body. "Mam? Mam?"

A lone man arrived, he glanced down. "I'll fetch yer Da. Remain here."

She sat on the ground for a long time, her hand on her

mother's chest, willing her to breathe.

By the time her father and another man arrived, the sun had fallen, and Leana was shaking so hard from the cold that she could not speak.

They'd buried her mother under a tree that they could see from the front door. Her father's grief had been crippling. He didn't go anywhere for weeks. It was only due to the kindness of people in the village that they had food.

Leana's grief was different. Instead of crying, she'd remained silent for many weeks. Only nodding or shaking her head when spoken to.

Now almost ten years later, whenever she looked out to the tree where her mother rested, the need to once again be silent fell over her.

"LEANA, HOW FARES yer Da?" Athol, The constable walked toward her, the easygoing man doing his best to remain a short distance. He'd been one of the men who'd helped bury her mother and for it, she'd always been grateful.

"He is healing."

They walked away from others in the market to a table and two chairs outside the tavern where the constable often held court.

After Athol motioned for her to sit, Leana lowered into a chair and placed her basket on the ground next to her feet.

"I hear Ross men are helping ye and yer Da. Is there more that can be done?"

Leana shook her head. "Nay."

"Will the warriors complete all the work?" The constable sat back, seeming at ease.

"As ye know, Gawyn took all our coin. The laird is giving us coin to pay for a few men to finish what the warriors can't do in a sennight. Father gave a list to one of the warriors of four names of those who can do the work."

The constable ignored what she said about hiring men. "Speaking of Gawyn. It is strange that he would leave without speaking to his family. Ye are well aware of how close that family is."

Leana wanted to scream. Why did everyone care so much about a person whose departure should be a celebration? Gawyn was a horrible unkind person.

"I do not know what happened to Gawyn. He is a thief and a liar, he ran because he probably did something and did nae wish to be caught."

The constable looked toward the market, and it was then Leana noticed that Willa and one of her brothers stood watching the interaction between her and Athol.

"Did he leave anything behind?"

Leana was struck silent by the question. "He took some clothes, his cloak, and our coin." She leaned toward the constable. "Father wishes him to return so that he can demand Gawyn pay back what he stole."

"I believe ye."

"Will ye speak to them?" Leana looked toward where Willa continued watching.

"Aye," the constable replied. "Go with care."

Ensuring to give Willa a wide berth, Leana hurried to complete her purchases. The most important being herbs for her father's pain.

Not wishing to linger too long, she walked back to the edge

of the village. Just as she was past the chapel, Willa's brother, Tom, stepped out from behind the building.

"Weaving lies about my brother are ye?"

Tom was quite large, seeming to grow rounder every year. Although Leana had not had much interaction with him, she knew he was no better than Gawyn.

Remaining quiet, Leana took a step back.

"Admit that ye and yer father did something to my brother. Ye should both hang." Tom spit on the ground. "Do I have to beat the truth out of ye?"

Leana turned on her heel and raced to the other side of the chapel and into the forest. She doubted the rotund man could catch her, so she wasn't too worried.

After a while, she finally slowed and looked over her shoulder.

The forest was quiet as the birds and other beasts took note of her running and silenced to see what was about. There were also no sounds of anyone following her.

It would not be much longer before she arrived home, however, upon emerging from the forest, there was a patch of road that she'd not have anywhere to hide.

She stopped by a tree allowing her body to settle and her breathing to normalize. How had she ever thought herself to be in love with Gawyn? It was the mistake of a naïve lass that she now paid dearly for.

After taking her virginity, he'd adamantly refused to marry her. She'd lied to her father and told him they'd been married by the local vicar. From the moment he moved into their home, Gawyn had been unkind to both her and her father. Always putting them down. Worst of all he refused to do any work on the farm.

If ever she contradicted him, she'd been met with a back-handed slap, or grips so hard they'd left dark bruises on her arms.

The daydreams of a naïve lass had become a yearlong nightmare. If only she'd listened to her father and been obedient enough to stay away from Gawyn Smith.

WHEN SHE MADE it home, the warriors were winding down from work and the same group of people had arrived with food and drink.

Leana walked to Beth Mackinnon, a farmer's wife and her only female friend. The woman was walking around collecting bowls as the men finished eating and handing out small berry pies, much to the warrior's delight.

"Beth, ye are such a dear to do this for us. I can never repay yer kindness." Leana took the dirty bowls. "I will wash them."

Her friend caught up with her. "I fed yer father as well. He seems to be in pain. Ye should boil the herbs for him."

"Aye, I will." Leana looked toward where the warriors ate, her gaze clashing with Torac's who looked up just then.

She let out a breath. "I can make the meal for tomorrow."

The woman nodded good-naturedly. "I will come and help ye, if ye wish. Feeding the grateful men has given me a reason to smile upon waking." Beth's only daughter had married and although her sons still lived at home, she complained about not having anything to do.

"Then ye can continue to do what ye wish," Leana said smiling at her.

"Ye were gone a bit longer than usual. Did something

happen?" Beth asked.

Leana told her about going to the market and being questioned by the constable and taunted by Tom. "I had to run most of the way back."

"At least ye know the boar of a man would never attempt to run," Beth replied. "Did ye purchase the herbs? Yer father will be glad for it tonight."

"He would be in much less pain if he remained still," Leana said, looking to where her father stood leaning on a home-made crutch while speaking to a warrior.

Her blood went cold at Willa appearing. The woman's eyes narrowed at both her and Beth before she made a beeline for Torac.

"I am surprised that she comes here," Beth whispered.

"It is only because the warriors are here. She is repeating to anyone who will listen that Father and I have something to do with Gawyn disappearing."

Beth let out a breath. "And no doubt comes here in hopes of finding a husband."

Raindrops began falling and Leana hoped it meant Willa would leave. The woman was not a stranger to flirting. Having been married until her husband was killed during a clash with other villagers.

Willa had been seeking to remarry as soon as her mourning time was over.

After her experience with Gawyn, Leana did not understand the need to have a man in one's life, especially not a husband. A cruel man could make a woman's life horrible.

Her gaze drifted to Torac, who looked on as Willa spoke. He didn't seem cruel at all, quite the opposite. There was a quiet gentleness about him that set her at ease.

Leana gave Beth a knowing look at Willa's mannerisms.

Willa clutched in front of her chest and spoke with a soft expression. Anyone who knew the woman would laugh at her attempt to seem demure.

It was only when the rain began to fall harder, that Willa and another woman, who came with her, finally hurried home.

Too busy following Willa's progress, Leana wasn't aware Torac had neared until he spoke. "Ye should get out of the rain," he said.

Beth chuckled. "Leana and I often work in the rain. If we sought shelter each time it did, nothing would get done."

With a slight curve to the corners of his lips, he guided them to under the roof's overhang. "My men and I will sleep in the stables tonight. It looks as if it will rain all night."

"Please do. Ye do not have to stay outdoors at all," Leana replied, annoyed at the breathlessness of her voice.

His gaze met hers for a beat longer than necessary and Leana felt her cheeks warm before he looked to Beth. "The food was very good. Thank ye."

This time Beth flushed. "I am grateful for the peace ye, and yer men have brought to the region."

"There are still the robbers that we seek, but aye, it is much more peaceful." Torac shrugged. "I best get things situated. We should be finished with at least half of the field in a pair of days."

When he walked away, Beth nudged Leana. "He is very handsome. I have never stood that near a man so large. All of the warriors are so...well-built."

"Let us not forget they are built for battle and death,"

Leana said while scanning the other men who carried things into the stables. "Although, they seem to be conscious of their intimidating demeanor and do well to keep their distance."

Beth nodded. "Aye, I agree. I would not like come upon that lot if I were up to no good."

WHEN BETH LEFT and her father was resting, it was time for Leana to finish her duties.

She took the bucket of leftovers from the day's meal and fed the pigs, then she looked after the chickens and the goats. There would be no time that day to see about the garden, however, she picked a few vegetables that were ripe.

"Ye should rest."

Torac's voice made her jump. Leana turned to find that he studied her with interest.

"I could say the same to ye," she replied boldly. Although her hand shook a bit, Leana managed to place the items in her basket before straightening.

"Before yer husband's disappearance were ye always as busy?" He looked from her to the garden and then to the pens.

"Gawyn was never much help. Father and I have always done all the work required. Besides feeding and caring for the animals, I garden, cook, and take care of the house. There are moments when I sit and sew, times of rest."

"I have wondered about…" He frowned. "What I wish to do when I no longer fight."

Leana's eyes widened. "Ye are a warrior through and through. It is hard to imagine ye doing anything else."

"Aye,"—he shrugged—"I cannot fight forever."

The fact she was comfortable having a conversation with

Torac, was not lost on Leana. She studied his face. "What do ye think ye would like to do?"

"Live somewhere like here. Open. Not in a village or the keep. I would like to spend time with horses and…" He left the rest unsaid, seeming to become flustered.

Leana motioned to the garden. "It would be possible to maintain a small parcel and be self-sufficient. There is nothing more father and I need that we cannot barter or trade for when there is not enough coin.

"I have saved most of my earnings. Like most warriors who are without a family, I have little need for coin."

"Ye have finely made clothes."

Torac's eyebrow lifted. "Ye noticed?"

At the comment, Leana's face burned bright. Obviously he teased her, but she was not at all used to a man doing so and she was lost on how to respond. "I-I… It is obvious ye care about it…"

"Leana." The way he said her name was as if he touched her and shivers ran down from her chest to her stomach. Something fluttered there and she placed a hand over it.

"Aye?"

She was fully aware of his nearing, of what would occur, but Leana was totally helpless. Her body was still, her lips parted to allow breath, and her eyes locked to his mouth as it came closer.

When he pressed his lips to hers, Leana's eyes fell closed at the wonderful sensation of his kiss. It was as if any necessity to think, move, or breathe was gone. Leana lifted her hand, her fingers pressing to his unshaven jaw.

Then it ended. She let out a long breath and opened her

eyes to see that Torac walked away.

Her breath caught. How had it happened? That a man was able to get close enough to kiss her. Not only that, but she'd reached for him in return.

Leana raced to the house, yanked the door open, and flew inside pulling it firmly behind. Back pressed against the solid wood of the door was the only way she could keep from sinking to the floor.

Ever so slowly, she lifted her finger to touch her lips and found they curved into a soft smile.

CHAPTER FIVE

"I S SHE THE reason we are here?" Balgair's expression was unreadable, but there was a twinkle in his gaze. "She is bonnie."

"She is," Torac said walking past to find the place where he'd laid his blanket. Unfortunately, Balgair followed. "What do ye plan to do about it?"

After folding his tartan over the blankets, it was much more comfortable. Torac rolled his other clothes to use as a pillow for his head. "I do not plan to do anything."

Balgair also prepared his bedding, the large man seeming at odds with how perfectly he folded and set everything. "There has been a change about ye recently."

"Change?" Torac couldn't help that his heart seemed to increase its pace. Was it obvious that he'd been having thoughts of leaving? "What do ye mean?"

The other warrior met his gaze. "Restless."

"As it is with each place we go. After the first months of so much to do, we settle into a way of doing each day that becomes like each day before. It may be time for me to go elsewhere."

"Or do something else."—Balgair's large shoulders lifted and lowered—"Ye and I are getting older. We have to consider that soon we will be more of a hindrance than help to the guard."

Warriors who worked for the laird, upon reaching a certain age were normally relegated to duties at the keep. Patrolling the walls and the interior of the house was not a bad way to live, however, Torac had no desire to do it.

"There is always the wall," Torac said as a joke, but his tone came across as bitter.

Balgair chuckled. "Not for me."

"What do ye plan to do after?" Torac asked, turning to look at Balgair.

"I will go to the seashore and build a small cottage. I will marry a willing wench. Spend my days fishing and my nights fucking."

The men around them laughed at the statement. Some joined in to tell Balgair it was a splendid plan.

Torac did not laugh, in truth, it sounded like a perfect life.

THE NEXT DAY the men were ready to get to work. They'd gotten used to the rhythm of what had to be done. Just one more day and they'd return to camp. Some looked forward to it, others said they were comfortable there at the MacKern farm.

When it came time for the meal, Torac washed up with water from the well. Leana worked diligently, setting out the bowls on a table that a neighboring family had brought. Her friend Beth smiled and waved at him then hurried into the house.

"Will ye return and check on... my father?" Leana asked not meeting his gaze. "It would be appreciated...by him."

"What of ye? Would ye like it if I came back to visit?"

She inhaled sharply, her cheeks pinkening. "I am afraid of what will happen. The talk of us harming Gawyn is worrisome," she said evading the question.

Just then Beth returned with a tray of cups. "Please call the men to eat. The food is hot and ready."

Torac wondered about the woman's home life, that she'd rather be there at the farm than at her own home. She seemed happy enough though.

"We are thankful for what ye do for us."

Beth motioned for him to go fetch the others with a warm look that said she appreciated his words. "I love keeping busy and helping Leana."

After the meal, once again other people arrived. More out of curiosity as they did not bring anything of note. Not in the mood to be around more people, Torac went to the nearby woods to both relieve himself and get some quiet time.

The quiet of the woods, with only an occasional rustling of leaves as the wind flowed through them was instantly calming. Birds scrambled from branch to branch seeming to search for the perfect place, their songs floating down as if for his ears alone.

Torac watched as two squirrels scampered around until their curious gazes took him in, and they hurried to the safety of their nest.

At the sound of a branch snapping, Torac whirled to find Willa pushing back a branch to walk past.

"I wondered where ye were," she informed him walking closer until he could reach out and touch her.

"Needed a bit of time to think." He hoped she'd make an excuse and leave. Instead, she smiled up at him.

"What troubles could ye possibly have? Ye work for the laird. Have coin and are well-regarded by the villagers."

Instead of a reply, he studied the woman. She was attractive, with dark brown hair, large expressive eyes, and was rather well endowed. However, Willa had a disposition that put him on alert. She was like a sly fox, wily and cunning.

"Has it been a long time since ye lay with a woman?"

The bold question brought a chuckle to his lips.

"Are ye offering?"

One step closer, she lifted her hands and cupped his face. "What if I am?"

"Then I would have to be a gentleman and refuse. Ye deserve more than a tumble in the woods." He hoped his words were convincing. Something told him she was not someone he'd want as an enemy.

Just then a gasp made them both turn. Leana stood stock-still taking them in. Her hand clutching the branches that she'd pushed aside.

"I apologize. Yer men asked about ye, and I offered to come and fetch ye." Leana whirled around and dashed away.

"Daft girl," Willa murmured, obviously bothered that at Leana's interruption, Torac had taken the opportunity to move away.

"Let us go back." Torac motioned for her to walk ahead of him. He was glad for Leana's interruption, but what she was sure to presume had been happening was bothering him.

UPON RETURNING TO the farm, Torac went in search of Leana. Despite the fact there wasn't anything between them, he wished to explain to her nothing had occurred between him and Willa.

After knocking on the door, Eli called for him to enter. Torac walked into the tidy room to find the man sitting up with his broken leg propped up on a stool.

"I am glad ye came in. Would ye care for something to drink?" Eli motioned to a shelf upon which sat a bottle. Torac retrieved it and then two cups from the kitchen. Leana was nowhere to be seen and he wondered if she'd run off to her bedchamber when he'd knocked.

The whiskey was oaky and smooth. Torac was impressed after expecting a burning concoction with little flavor.

"Ye and yer men will always have a place to stop and eat or lay yer heads," Eli began. "What ye have done for me, I can never repay." The man blinked away the moisture in his eyes. "Leana and I would have had a very sparse winter without yer help."

"We will ensure all is stored away before we leave tomorrow," Torac said standing.

Through the front window, he spotted Leana standing by a tree. "I will speak to yer daughter and ensure she knows who will be coming to help in the next day or two," Torac said by way of explanation in case the man saw him approaching Leana.

When he rounded the house, the wind picked up, blowing his hair sideways across his face. He'd not bothered to see about it in a long time and it needed to be trimmed. There would be time enough once he returned to camp.

At his approach, Leana did not react. Before her was a wooden grave marker. It was her mother.

"Since the work is almost complete, two of the men have

already returned to camp. Balgair, the other guard, and I will be leaving tomorrow. There is no need to plan to feed us.

She turned to him, seeming reluctant to lift her gaze to him. "I thought ye would be here another full day."

"We will be nearby if ye need us." There was a long moment of silence, neither of them moving.

Torac spoke again. "In the forest earlier. Nothing was going to happen."

"There is no need for ye to explain. Ye are free to do what ye wish." The words were barely above a whisper.

"But I want ye to know. I am not interested in Willa. She approached me..."

Leana met his gaze. "I prefer not to speak about it."

"The farmer from across the fields,"—Torac raised his arm and pointed in the direction—"his sons along with a man from the village will be coming to finish the work."

"He is Beth's husband. Their sons are always willing to help."

"After a sennight, whatever needs to be done, has to be paid by yer father, on the promise of payment once the wheat is sold. They agreed to work as long as it is needed to harvest the entire field."

Looking in the direction he pointed, Leana nodded. "They are kind people."

"I believe most people are," Torac replied, his mind scrambling for how to prolong the conversation. "What do ye truly believe happened to Gawyn?"

He wanted to know more about the man who could possibly return at any moment. If her husband was alive, then Leana was not free to pursue a relationship with anyone.

At the same time, he wondered if perhaps the reason she and her father were aware the man was dead.

"I believe he and his band of bullies did something and they were killed. Although no one will say it, it is common knowledge they were the ones who cause many of the troubles around here."

"Such as?"

"I believe them to be the ones who attacked the family south of here last spring. Although he never explained, the burn mark across the left side of his face was because of it."

Torac's blood ran cold. "His face was burned?"

Leana nodded. "Aye. Fire left him with a disfiguring scar. He claimed it happened when he rolled into a campfire in his sleep, but I did not believe it."

His stomach tightened and Torac had to know more. "Did yer husband ever admit doing anything to ye?"

There was a flash in her gaze as if something about the question brought a reminder. "Nay. He did not."

"There are attacks on families all the time. If he were to be killed because of it…"

Leana shook her head. "Whatever happened to him— whether he was killed, or he just left—it does not matter, does it?" Her brows gathered together. "Actions bring consequences. However, that said, I do not wish Gawyn dead."

"I will return to see about ye Leana," Torac told her. Then before she could react, he pressed a soft kiss to her lips.

As he walked away, he could feel her gaze on his back. Then upon looking to the window, he noted Eli watching him without expression.

Was it possible that the man whose face haunted him at

night was Gawyn Smith? Torac pushed the thought from his head. He would consider it another time. For now, it was best to plan for the day ahead.

THEY'D FINISHED PUTTING everything away, the horses were saddled and the last of their belongings in sacks. It was then that Eli came to the door to see them off.

The man once again thanked them profusely and wished them a safe journey. "Where will ye go today? Back to yer camp?"

"We will ride through Welland and then head back to the camp, aye," Torac replied referring to a nearby village.

THEY'D RIDDEN FOR a few hours, the sun was high in the sky, and thankfully it had not rained. Ahead a man on a horse came into view and Balgair exchanged a look with Torac and the other guard to ensure they saw him.

When the rider drew closer, they realized it was a young lad. "The farm over there," he said breathlessly. "They were attacked."

At once, the warriors urged their horses into a gallop, slowing only upon seeing a cottage in flames and a man running from it.

The young lad caught up and pointed. "They went toward the woods."

"We will see about the family first." Upon arriving at the burning home, Torac hurried to the man, who limped as he rushed to the stables to open the doors.

"Is there anyone in the house?" Torac called out.

The man shook his head, his face anxious. "My wife, daughter and sons are there." He pointed to three people ushering pigs and goats from a pen that was too close to the fire.

Once the family was assured their livestock was safe, it was only then that the man comforted his wife. Torac's heart broke at the soot-stained faces of the family, who were left with no more than what they wore.

A trio of men, who were neighboring farmers, rode up on horseback and asked what they could do to help. Moments later, a pair of wagons arrived. Women climbed down and hurried to the still grieving family.

"They are fortunate to have the community," Balgair said. "Soon the house will be rebuilt, and they will go on with their life."

Torac looked past the people to where a few animals and a horse lay on the ground nearby, obviously, they'd not made it out in time.

He stormed up to where the farmer spoke to the others. "Who did this?"

The man shrugged and shook his head.

"It is a group of men who've been tormenting us. They demand coin and when we do not pay, they do this," another farmer replied.

Another nodded. "No good bastards, they are. Come from Welland and Aldress." He shook his fist. "We have gone in search of them several times, but they are adept at hiding. And keep their faces covered."

The men began discussing what they'd seen. One spoke of

a horse with a recognizable mark. A white circle on the rump.

"My men and I will go search," Torac said. "How many were there?"

The farmer wiped his face with a rag. It only smeared the soot more. "There were four. Perhaps five."

"Very well."

"We will help the family. Do not fash," a farmer said. "We take care of our own."

"That is good to hear," Torac replied.

"WE SHOULD RETURN to camp and get more men," the warrior told him and Balgair. "There may be more men than the farmer saw."

Balgair shook his head. "If they are intimidating people in order to make coin, there cannot be more than four or five. The people here do not have much."

"True, the more thieves the less each man gets," Torac replied, fury coursing through him. Of all the things that he disliked, thieves were near the top of his list.

They arrived at an area past the small village of Alness that they rarely patrolled.

"Best we slow. We are not as familiar with these lands, neither are the people here used to us," Balgair said looking from the ground up to the trees. "Seems desolate."

"If there are no people about, there may be a reason," Torac said.

They rode a while longer until coming to a shallow stream. They stopped to allow the horses to drink all the while keeping an eye out for anyone who approached.

Other than an occasional call from a bird, the area remained eerily silent. Torac thought to have entered a magical realm, but for the strange lack of sounds.

Out of the corner of his eye he caught movement and automatically clutched the hilt of his sword. His companions did the same only to relax when a doe and her young appeared. The mother kept an eye on them while her young drank, then daring a short drink they darted away into the woods.

"We can camp here," Balgair said. "No one will approach without us hearing."

Torac was not as accepting of the situation. "I do not think it is a good idea to sleep somewhere like here. If it is silent, it is because something is afoot."

A flock of birds flew into a nearby tree, their loud chirps breaking the silence as they seemed to argue over who was to settle where.

"It is a good place. We are near water, have the shelter of trees in case of rain, and like Balgair said, if someone approaches, we will hear them."

"Not if the wee bastards do not quiet down," one of the warriors said narrowing his gaze at the tree full of birds.

THE SNAPPING OF a twig alerted Torac to someone or something approaching. Although he lay atop his bedroll, he'd kept his sword close at hand. By the time he shook the heaviness of sleep away, attackers were upon them.

Balgair and another warrior had awakened at the same time, but like him, he were not quite as alert as those who rushed toward them.

The fight was short as the men who'd come had probably expected them to be hunters and not experienced warriors.

Dragging an injured man, they'd run away only moments after arriving.

Torac and a pair of warriors gave chase only to lose them as the men knew the area and could easily hide.

"Bastards! Where is Thomas?" Torac screamed to the others. The young warrior was to have been on patrol.

Just then he saw Thomas' body slumped over next to a tree, his throat cut.

"Where's Balgair?" Torac asked walking back.

Caelan, an archer, let out a breath. "I believe he stayed back at the camp." They looked at each other and raced back to find Balgair on his knees clutching his side.

"The bastards got me. How is that possible?"

"We were outnumbered," the warrior said. "And asleep."

Balgair groaned. "Ye do not make me feel better."

While they spoke, Torac fed wood to the fire to better see the wound. It was a deep gash on Balgair's left side. It bled quite profusely and soon it was obvious Balgair was about to pass out.

Tearing his tartan, Torac, and the warrior wrapped Balgair's waist tightly. The poor man could barely keep from crying out from the pain.

"Get on yer horse," Torac commanded. "Ye are too large for us to do it without hurting ye worse."

With torches in hand, they retraced their path back to Aldress. The entire time Torac wondered if Balgair would make it without falling from his steed.

CHAPTER SIX

RUNNING. LEGS BURNING. Leana could barely catch her breath as she raced through the trees, ignoring the branches that lashed out at her, scratching her face and arms.

The laughter told her that her pursuers were not too far behind. She didn't dare to turn and look as it would slow her progress.

"We will get ye, lass," one of them called out. He sounded out of breath, which was good. It meant they, like her, he was tiring. Unlike them, she had the added strength that came from fear.

Since Gawyn's disappearance, she'd had to put up pair of unruly young lads from the village, sent by Tom and Willa, to get her to admit that she knew where Gawyn was. Leana was well aware that if they caught her, they would not stop just at questioning her.

She tripped on a branch, crying out in pain as she fell forward onto the ground. Somehow, Leana managed to scramble to her feet and run toward a road. She prayed the farmer or one of his sons would be near the edge of the fields and see her.

The cowards who chased her would not continue if there were witnesses. At least that is what she hoped.

At the yanking of her hair pulling her back, Leana let out a scream. She turned toward her assailant scratching, kicking, and biting with what little strength she had left.

The barking of dogs made everyone stop and listen. Moments later, hounds broke through the trees, two large hunting dogs.

Her assailants moved away, stepping back slowly, holding their hands out to keep the dogs at bay. One pulled a knife ready to fight if one attacked. The dogs snarled, the low growls sending shivers of fear up Leana's spine. Thankfully, the beasts were too focused on the four men to pay her any mind.

As slowly as possible, she got to her feet and walked backwards.

"Do not worry," a woman's voice said. A hooded figure appeared. The woman spared only a glance to the lads, who continued backing away, the dogs moving with them.

"My dogs will not hurt ye," the woman said to Leana. "Them, however, I must decide what to do about."

The attacker with the knife narrowed his eyes at the woman. "Call off yer hounds or I will kill them."

"That I doubt," the woman replied. "Be on yer way. If ye turn back, my hounds will hear ye."

"Come lads," she said, and the dogs instantly returned and stood at her side. It was then Leana finally felt somewhat safe.

There was a rustle of leaves, intermittent cursing, and footsteps as her assailants fled.

"Wh-why did ye l-let them go?" Leana asked breathlessly. She bent at the waist and took long breaths. "Th-they will return t-to chase me."

Leana had heard stories of the woman and her hounds. She was called Swannoc and had only recently come to the area.

From what was said, she'd been aboard a ship that had sunk off the southern shore and had lost her husband and children.

"Why do ye walk the wood alone if ye are in danger?" The woman's green gaze met hers. "At least find yerself a hound or something to protect ye." Her gaze moved to her dogs. "It is what I did. I have no need of a man, prefer my own company."

"I should," Leana said finally getting her breath back. "I went to the village for herbs. I should have asked someone to go with me or taken the wagon and gone the long way. Now I have neither the herbs nor the basket and bring back cuts and bruises instead."

Leana let out a shaky breath. "Why must men be so horrible?"

"I will walk ye home," Swannoc said, not replying to her question, as there was no answer.

They walked slowly as Leana was too tired to attempt a quick pace. She studied the dogs that trotted alongside. "Where were ye going?"

"I am a healer and forage for certain things near here. I heard yer scream." Swannoc turned to Leana. "I saw warriors at yer home, what happened?"

As they continued, Leana told her about her father's injury and about Gawyn's disappearance. It was an easy rapport between them, and Leana hoped they would become friends. "Would ye like to come in and meet my father?" Leana asked when they neared her home.

"Perhaps another day," Swannoc replied. "I must return to my own home. Be with care."

"Swannoc?" Leana stopped her. "Can ye help me find a hound or two?"

The woman chuckled. "Of course." One of the dogs growled and Swannoc turned to it. She narrowed her eyes and looked around.

As soon as she entered, Leana knew something was wrong. Her father's face was pale, and he looked from her to the other side of the room where Tom stood with a furious expression.

"Tell me what happened to Gawyn."

Leana lost her temper. She'd had enough of it. With hands clenched, she closed the distance between them. "I do not know how many times I must tell ye that Father and I have no knowledge of where he went. He took our coin and left one morning. Leave us be."

The man huffed. "Ye both know where he is. Did ye kill him and bury him? Where?"

"Ye can ask as much as ye want," her father interjected, getting to his feet. "The answer will remain the same. It is the truth."

Rage roared through her at the reddening on her father's left cheek. The man had struck him.

"Instead of being intent on us, ye should be searching for him," Leana screamed. "Leave us be!"

Just then Swannoc and her dogs appeared in the doorway. "Leave or I will set them on ye."

Tom had the audacity to chuckle and said to Leana, "Ye are not a good liar." With that, he turned and walked out the back door pushing her sideways as he passed.

"Father," she said as she hurried over to him as he lowered himself into a chair. "I will get ye some water."

"What happened?" He studied her face.

"A boar chased me in the woods." The lie came easily as

she didn't wish to worry her father further.

When she looked to the doorway, Swannoc was gone. Hopefully to ensure Tom went home this time.

"I wish Gawyn had never come into our lives. Whatever made Willa bring it all up again, I cannot know. What I do know is that it has to stop."

After washing up, Leana cooked a simple meal. As they ate, she told her father about the woman Swannoc and her hounds.

"I saw her once," her father said. "She is very independent for a woman. Seems fearless."

"No one is fearless," Leana said. "I do agree she is brave."

Her father felt well enough to help with the feeding of the pigs and chickens. Meanwhile, Leana milked the cows and saw about hay for the goats. They worked until sundown when she was to the point of falling from exhaustion.

And yet sleep did not claim her. Leana thought back to the day Gawyn left. Was there something she'd missed?

"I HAVE SOMEWHERE to go. Fetch Mackinnon's sons to help with work for the next few days."

"We cannot afford to pay them," Leana whispered so her father would not hear. "Ye are well aware of it. Ye have called them to work too many times already."

He gave her one of his annoyed looks. "What use are ye?" He sat up in the bed, looking around. Often when on the brink of a fight, he did this, looked for a reason to argue.

Leana diverted his attention. "Where are ye going?"

"To gather more coin than ye've ever seen."

"Alone?"

He mumbled a reply and she strained to hear the words.

What had he said?

LEANA SAT UP, unable to see in the darkness. There was no moon, which made the interior of her room pitch black other than a bit of a flicker in the hearth. She went to the fireplace and stuck a twig into the embers until it caught and then lit a candle.

He'd said, *with my brother.* She was sure of it. Why then did Tom insist on getting an answer from them?

Had Gawyn not made it to their meeting point? She paced the room wondering what had actually happened that day.

POUNDING ON THE door woke her the next morning and she hurried to see who it was. Her father emerged from his side of the house. "Warriors," he said.

Outside there were a group of warriors, one stood closer waiting for someone to open the door.

Her father hobbled to the door and opened it, with Leana standing just behind. "What can I do for ye?"

"I am called Struan and am seeking Torac and his men. They were to have returned to camp by now."

Leana's eyes widened. "They left two days ago. Torac said they were headed to Aldness then back to the guard post."

The man Struan nodded. "Was anything amiss when they left?"

Her father shook his head. "Nay, they left early in the morning. Said they wished to reach Aldness and then be back to camp by nightfall."

The warriors thanked them, refusing drink or food, and mounted. The thundering of the huge mount's hooves vibrated the ground as they rode away.

"What could have happened?" Leana asked, her heart racing. "There were only four of them. Perhaps they ran into the men who are causing all the trouble."

Her father shook his head. "Let us hope they are unharmed."

"Father?" Leana said. "I had a dream last night that woke me."

"I wondered why ye were pacing by candlelight," her father replied with a warm look.

A long sigh left her. "I do not know if it was the dream or a memory, but the morning Gawyn left, he said he was going with his brother."

"Tom?"

"Aye. I asked who he was traveling with and Gawyn said, "my brother", I could swear it."

They sat in silence for a bit.

"If that is true, then why is he so persistent?"

"He may know what happened and wants to shift blame. Does not want the family to scorn him for it."

Going back to the window, she peered out. "I best go see about the chores."

Her mind went to Torac. Where was he?

If only there was a way to find out.

CHAPTER SEVEN

U PON WAKING, BALGAIR opened his eyes and tried to sit. The pain instantly reminding him of why he was in the strange room.

It had been days, he wasn't sure how long since arriving there. Torac and the other warrior had been there and gone. He seemed to recall them returning on occasion, but he'd not been able to speak. Much too ravaged with pain and fever, all he'd been able to do was try to fight against allowing the tide of darkness to take him away.

A woman loomed over him, the bright green eyes studying his. "I see ye have decided to join the living," she said without any sort of inflection.

When he tried to speak, his throat constricted. He managed to whisper, "Water."

The woman brought a cup to his lips and lifted his head so that he could drink. He gulped down the contents and closed his eyes. "It was but a cut," he managed to say.

"Deep. And ye lost a great deal of blood. The wound became festered, which is why ye have been fevered."

At her words, he ran his hand down the injured side. He was bandaged, but from what he could feel through the bandages, the wound was larger than he remembered.

"We had to cut away some flesh. The wound will take a

long time to heal." Again, she spoke as if it were nothing more than a splinter. "Ye are strong, I am sure ye will recover in yer own good time."

Balgair let out a breath and this time managed to sit up using his elbows to keep upright. "I must go. I have coin to pay ye."

The woman straightened to her full height, and he had to admit if not for the pain and not knowing where Torac and the others were, he'd be interested in getting to know her. With long reddish hair and bright green eyes, she was a beauty. From her flat-footed stance and arms loose on her sides, he guessed she was a fighter. Perhaps not a warrior, but someone who could defend themselves. The only ones who stood like her were guards and warriors.

"If ye try to stand and fall on the floor I will leave ye there," she stated. "Perhaps in a day or two, ye can try."

"Where are the men who brought me?"

"They come every day. I am sure before sunset, they will be here to see about ye." She turned to walk away.

"I am called Balgair. Who are ye?"

Her eyes met his and she hitched her chin a bit. "I am a healer, we are in my home near Aldness. They were taking ye there when ye fell off the horse. I was walking by and offered to help."

She'd not told him her name and Balgair would not ask again. It was her home and she'd taken care of him. So she owed him nothing.

"Thank ye," he said acknowledging that perhaps she was right. He lowered back onto the bed and closed his eyes.

"Swannoc is my name."

The aroma of food woke him next and by the light through the window, it was late afternoon. Balgair moved slowly and tried to sit, his breath catching at the pain of every movement. After a moment, he gave up.

Would he be able to fight again? If they had to cut flesh, it meant a long healing process.

Interesting that not that long ago, he and Torac had the conversation about what they'd do when no longer warriors. Now perhaps his own time had come to consider a different life.

Swannoc entered with a tray, upon it a bowl and a cup. "It is rabbit stew."

She placed the tray on a side table and came closer. "I will help ye to sit. Use yer legs and back, try not to move yer midsection."

Following her instructions of swinging his legs to the side of the bed and using his left elbow, Balgair sat up with less pain than before.

While he ate, she stood by the window looking out. "Yer friends arrive. Others are with them."

She made a whistling sound and two large hunting dogs rushed to her side. Swannoc turned to him. "My dogs are not kind to strangers."

The hounds barely paid Balgair any mind, except for one who sniffed the air and took a step toward the bed.

"No," Swannoc said in a stern tone and the hound returned to her side. "The warriors will be glad to see that ye are up." With that, she walked out, the hounds at her side.

MOMENTS LATER, TORAC and Struan entered. Both seemed

surprised that he was up and eating.

"I am glad to see ye awake," Torac said. "I wondered if ye would die."

Balgair shook his head. "I considered it. Remember waking one night in so much pain, death would have been easier."

The archer, Struan looked from Balgair to Torac. "I was sent to see about ye when none of ye returned. Why did ye not send Caelan?" he asked.

"Because we do not know where the men who attacked us are and if attacked he could have been killed," Torac explained.

Balgair barely stopped holding up a spoonful of the delicious food to speak. "Are ye going to hunt them down?"

"We return to camp," Struan said. "Once there, we will return with more men and begin looking for them."

"When do we leave?"

Torac and Struan exchanged looks. "Ye have not seen the wound?" Torac asked.

His stomach sank. It must have been worse than he expected by Torac's expression.

"It matters not. I will not remain here." Balgair stopped eating, his appetite gone. "There is no need for me to stay."

"We leave first thing. There is no time to find a cart." Struan looked anywhere but at him while speaking.

"Then I will mount." Balgair wasn't sure why he continued to argue. It was more than evident they did not think he could. Stubborn as he was, even sitting up was costing him.

Swannoc came to the doorway. "I must clean his wound while ye are here."

"I will help," Torac said, and Struan walked out.

It was then Balgair noted that Swannoc held a bucket and a basket. Torac took the bucket of water and brought it closer to the bed, while Swannoc placed bandages and a knife on the bedside table. By their movements, it wasn't the first time they'd done this and Balgair wondered if they'd developed a friendship.

Torac met his gaze. "If ye are finished." When Balgair nodded, he took the tray of uneaten food.

In silence the bandages were cut off and Balgair took a deep breath before looking down. His entire left side was mangled, the flesh pulled and stitched shut in some places in others the wound gaped open.

A foul odor assaulted as he noticed seeping from just below his waist.

The room began to spin, and he gulped, doing his best not to throw up the bit of food he'd just eaten. It wasn't as if he'd not witnessed death. In fact, he'd caused it many times. He knew and understood the length of a dead body by smell.

His wound smelled of death.

"Ye must lay on yer unharmed side," Swannoc instructed and with Torac's help, he managed it. After crossing his arm over his chest, she began rinsing the wound. If asked, he would not be able to describe whether or not the cleansing and rebandaging were painful. His mind was gone the entire time as he came to grips with the fact that his life was forever changed.

Never again would he be able to raise a sword to defend Laird Ross.

THE NEXT MORNING, the warriors left without Balgair. They'd paid Swannoc more than she'd asked for in exchange for caring for their comrade. From the expressions, it was not an easy thing to leave the warrior behind, but any travel would kill the man.

Swannoc sat in her front room and gazed at the room where Balgair slept. She'd given up her chamber and now slept in the front room. It didn't bother her, as many nights it was where she'd slept. The dogs scratched at the door, and she allowed them outside. They were loyal creatures and would not wander far.

At hearing a moan, she tensed and listened intently to see if Balgair called out for her. Instead, there was silence. Probably moving about had caused him pain.

Every time she saw his wound, Swannoc felt horrible for him. From what Torac told her, he was a fearsome warrior, who lived for battle. Now he would fight no more.

The festering had spread fast, and she'd barely stayed ahead of it. Even now, she worried it had begun again.

What if? She got up and hurried to the bed chamber and found him sitting up, staring out at the night sky.

"Are ye in pain?"

He didn't turn. "Am I to die?"

The deep timber of his voice was like a balm to her ears, reminding her of someone else. Swannoc went to the window and peered out. "I do not think so. Tomorrow, I may have to cut more flesh. I hope that I washed it well enough so that it heals."

When she met his gaze, he searched hers. The way he looked at her, as if she held all hope made her want to reach out to him. Other than for healing, she'd not touched a man since the shipwreck. She'd lost all desire in men.

Yet seeing the muscled warrior on the brink of losing his purpose, it touched her.

"When ye heal, only then should ye consider what is next. Our bodies are complex and wonderful. Capable of many miraculous things."

"I have no illusion of ever fighting again. Given time, acceptance will come." Once again he met her gaze. "Will ye help me to lay down please?"

Swannoc walked closer. "Lean to the uninjured side. Place yer elbow out to catch ye," she instructed him until he lay on his side and then she lifted his legs to the bed. After, Swannoc pulled the blankets up over him.

"Sleep well. In the morning things will seem better."

Their gazes connected, neither looking away and Swannoc smiled in what she hoped was a reassuring way.

"Ye as well," Balgair replied.

When she returned to the front room, the dogs were waiting. She undressed and climbed into a cot in front of the hearth. When she closed her eyes, she saw Balgair's face.

The man was ruggedly handsome and well-built. If not for her lack of interest in forming any kind of a relationship, she'd be very tempted.

With a huff, she rolled to her other side. What ridiculous thoughts one had late at night.

IT WAS ONE morning, a pair of days later, that Swannoc woke from an afternoon nap to a quiet house. She entered the bedchamber to find Balgair was gone.

Breath caught, she hurried back out only to then notice that her hounds were gone as well. If that man harmed even one hair on their heads, she would ensure he never recovered fully. Quite the opposite.

After grabbing her broom, she raced to the front door and opened it to find no one about. By now she could barely breathe with dread. The fast beats of her heart echoed in her ears as she yanked open the back door.

After each slow step, Balgair paused. He took the next one using a stick as a cane and this time hung his head as if waiting for the pain to abate. On both sides of him, the dogs kept watch, their gaze intent on his every movement.

That the hounds did not bark, or growl was strange. They were less trusting than Swannoc when it came to men. And yet, with infinite patience, they remained at Balgair's side as he painstakingly circled back toward the house.

At one point, he reached out to one of the hounds and the animal moved so that its head was directly under Balgair's palm. Swannoc shook her head. If the huge man fell, the poor dog would be unable to do more than run.

"What are ye doing?" Swannoc hurried to Balgair. "Come inside before ye fall. I cannot possibly help ye if that were to happen."

There was a playful glint in his gaze that she'd not seen before and unwillingly, at the same time, a flutter in her stomach.

"Come." She took his arm, and they slowly made their way up to the house. "What did ye do to bewitch my dogs?"

"All dogs like me." Balgair let out a puff of air. "I must move around. I will not heal lying in bed."

Swannoc's hands could not encircle his large bicep, the flexing of the muscles was more than a bit distracting.

"Do so in the house." She dropped her hands and stalked inside, leaving him to make the rest of the trek alone.

CHAPTER EIGHT

"**A**RE YE SURE?" her father asked again. "Beth and her husband will wonder why ye do not come."

Outside Beth's husband and son approached, guiding a wagon they'd use to transport her father back to their home for a festive evening.

Leana went to the door and opened it. "I am looking forward to an entire evening and most of tomorrow spent in peace and quiet. The men who came to help are finally done with the harvest. It has been one thing after the other. I do not think I can withstand going to a crowded house at the moment."

"Very well," her father said in a resigned tone. "If ye change her mind, ye can always come in the morning."

"I will come tomorrow, late afternoon, to fetch ye. I promise," Leana said placing a kiss on his cheek, smiling to reassure him when he hobbled to the door.

It took more conversation to convince the men, she preferred to remain home before finally they left with promises of saving food for her.

Leana let out a long breath and sunk into a chair with a wide smile. Quiet. Finally.

Before her father's injury, she spent many a day alone in the house, sewing, cleaning, and other things. She treasured those times.

Outside the wind was becoming quite loud and she peered out to see that the chickens rushed into their coop for shelter, whilst the other larger animals seemed unperturbed. Nonetheless, she grabbed an overcoat and went out to see about things.

First she ensured their mare was settled in the stables. The field horse, a stubborn old thing would remain outside. She'd leave the stable doors open, but it was doubtful he'd go inside. No matter the weather, the horse hated being confined.

By the time she ensured the goats and pigs were well, fat raindrops were beginning to fall. Thankfully, Beth's home was not too far, so it was very possible, her father was inside before the rain began falling.

After removing her wet dress, Leana fed the fire in the hearth and wrapped in a blanket, she settled in front of it wearing only a dry chemise. No one would be coming, it would be a waste to dress.

The animals were fine and had food to last, so she could remain inside the warm house for the rest of the day.

Leana must have fallen asleep because at the sounds of knocks on the door, she was startled awake. Heart pounding, she froze in place.

Thankfully, the windows were shuttered, and no one could peer inside. Except for the small window in the kitchen, where a tall person could peer through, she felt safe.

The second set of knocks seemed to vibrate. What if it was Tom or a lone traveler? It was best that she remain silent and pray they did not think the cottage empty and break the door in.

"Leana."

She whirled to the small kitchen window to see a pair of familiar eyes. "Can I use the stable?"

It was Torac.

"Aye, of course," she replied getting to her feet and wrapping the blanket tightly around herself.

"Tell yer father I am seeking a place to dry off. Can I stay in the stable until the storm passes?"

She walked to the kitchen. "Put yer steed in the stable and come to the back door."

"Thank ye." Torac disappeared.

Quickly as possible, Leana rushed to her bedchamber and grabbed a simple frock to put over her chemise. Then she ran her fingers through her hair and went to the back door.

"Can I borrow a blanket?" A drenched Torac asked, standing at the doorway dripping water on the floor.

Her hands trembled as she retrieved the same blanket she'd just been using and walked back to him. She could feel his gaze following her and for some reason, it was enjoyable. "I have cloths to throw on the floor. Remove yer boots and whatever else ye can."

To give him privacy, she went to the kitchen to retrieve a kettle of water and hurried to the hearth to hang it over the fire. That completed, she then added wood to stoke the flames and turned.

Torac had removed his trews and wrapped the blanket about his waist fastening it in place with his belt. Placing the boots to the side of the door, he then lifted off his tunic and other clothing. Turning to the door, he opened it and wrung out the clothes as best he could.

"Ye can use the drying rack," she said pointing to the

wooden rack by the hearth.

If he noticed her father was not there, he didn't mention it. In all probability, Torac thought him asleep in the other room.

"What are ye doing riding alone? It is not safe," Leana said pouring the heated water into a mug and adding some herbs to it. Then she sweetened the liquid with honey.

Torac took the cup and sat down. He shivered and she realized the blanket she'd given him was barely enough for his lower half.

He was built so differently than Gawyn. Every muscle of his arms, shoulders, and chest were defined and his stomach flat, with a light trail of hair that went from across his chest and down the center of his body.

Like the rest of him, his legs were also well-toned from all the riding. At once she recalled the day she'd caught him bathing. Despite the anguish of her father's injury, she'd been unable to ignore the man's beauty.

"I will get ye another blanket. Sit by the fire."

His deep chuckle was throaty. "Ye remind me of my mother when I went out into the rain."

"If left to yer own devices, most men would kill themselves before reaching the age of six." Leana retrieved a second blanket and placed it over his shoulders. The act seemed intimate, and she felt her cheeks warm.

To keep busy, she lowered to another chair near the fire and lifted her cup to drink.

"I was headed back to the guard camp with a group. I decided to divert and come see about ye...and yer father, of course." It was then he looked around as if seeking him.

"I see. It is kind of ye," Leana replied.

Torac leaned toward her, his hazel gaze darkening. "I did promise to come and see ye. In truth, I wish to court ye."

Panic rose. Leana's mouth fell open, but she could not think of what to say. Her father thought her married. Although Gawyn was gone, she was tied to him unless he was, in fact, dead.

Could she trust a man again? Allow someone to have so much control that when they became cruel there was nothing to be done about it. Like Torac, Gawyn had been so nice to her in the beginning. So much so that even though she'd never truly loved him, she'd become his lover. The necessity of having a man in her life had overridden common sense.

"I do not know what to say..." She swallowed at how hard a heated streak of arousal suddenly wove its way through her entire body, making it virtually impossible to reach for him. Instead, Leana clutched the mug in her hands hoping it didn't break from the hold.

"Say ye will consider it," Torac said.

"I best cook something." Leana practically jumped to her feet and hurried to the kitchen where she blindly grabbed some of the vegetables she'd gathered from the garden and began chopping them.

Oh, how, she wanted Torac. The desire to be with him was stronger than anything in her life. If only she could see what the future held and if he would remain kind.

"What is it?" Torac came up behind her, took the knife from her hand, and turned her toward him by the shoulders. "Tell me."

Afraid as she was of what would occur if she looked into his eyes, she slowly lifted her gaze. Doubt and perhaps fear were obvious as he peered down at her. The question in the air of whether or not she wanted him.

"Aye, I want ye. I do. I am just not sure if I will ever be able to trust again. With Gawyn, it was good. In the beginning…"

"I am not Gawyn," Torac said, teeth gritted. "I am not like him."

When Torac pulled her against him, it was as if every prayer was answered by the relief that flowed through Leana. She wanted to feel his body against hers, wanted his mouth, his touch, everything.

Their mouths clashed with the intensity of two long-lost lovers. Leana clung to his shoulders, then wrapped her arms around his neck, needing him closer. He trailed kisses across her lips, teasing the corners before going in the opposite direction. All the while his hands traveled down her back to her sides where he settled them on her hips.

"Leana," he murmured. "Be with me."

"Mmm." It was perfect timing. No one needed to ever know. Just once she would be with a man she burned for.

"Yer father," he whispered, the breathy words tickling her ear. "Can we go to the stable?"

Boldness overtook her and Leana trailed her mouth to his jawline and then suckled at his neck. Torac moaned in pleasure. "Father is gone to a celebration. I will fetch him on the morrow."

At the words, once again he took her mouth, Torac's tongue delving past her lips to explore. She was consumed with so much want that her knees waivered.

Torac lifted her easily, and with long strides took her to the bedchamber.

It was but a matter of seconds for them both to be devoid of clothing. Leana, wearing only a frock and the chemise. Him, just the one blanket as the one from across his shoulders lay on the floor in the other room.

"Make love to me," Leana said clinging to his shoulder. "I want to forget everything except for us."

They could not stop kissing while exploring each other's bodies with their hands. Leana marveled at the smoothness of his skin while enjoying his weight over her. Torac kissed a trail from her mouth, down the side of her face to the juncture of her neck and shoulder. There he nipped at the sensitive skin, then licked it making her shudder.

Ripples of heat trickled down her body pooling in between her legs where a fire burned hotter than the fire in the hearth. She wanted to scream that he take her, at the same time she wished for this moment to last forever.

Torac's hardness pressed into her thigh, and she reached down to caress his length. He hissed at the touch, his eyes closing as she wrapped her fingers around it.

Taking the tip of her left breast into his mouth, he circled the opposite nipple with the pad of his thumb. Torac certainly knew how to bring a woman to the brink of passion. Causing her to lose all control before actually making love.

While his mouth moved from one breast to another, his hand slid through the center of her sex. Her entire body became rigid in expectation.

Gawyn had never cared about her when they were together, this was a very different experience for Leana, and she pressed her head back onto the bedding losing herself in every touch and every caress.

"Come for me lass," he said into her ear just as his tongue circled around it. At the same time, Torac stroked the pearl between her legs, and she did just that.

A sense of urgency fell over her as every inch of her body reacted to the intimate touches. Leana moaned loudly, lifting her body just as a rush of pure light took her to flight.

Through the haze of her climax, Torac settled between her legs and drove into her prolonging her release until she thought she could not withstand it.

With every thrust of his body, she floated between a second release and the wonder of how well their bodies fit together.

His hoarse moans were like warm oil poured over her and Leana swore to remember the sound.

"Kiss...me," she gasped, and he did, covering her mouth with his, his tongue driving into her in the same rhythm that his body moved until he could no longer keep pace. He lifted up looking deep into her gaze, the pace of his plunges faster and faster.

"Yes! Yes!" Leana cried out, unable to bear it any longer. The threat of a second or was it a third release was so powerful, she both urged it on and feared it.

Grabbing each half of his bottom, she dug her nails into the flesh urging him to release so that she could plunge with him.

His last drive was so hard she slid up the bed, her head against the wall, but she didn't care because her body shattered as he called out, lost in his own ecstasy.

When Torac collapsed over her, Leana stroked his back, her eyes refusing to open as she committed every moment to memory.

They were both drenched in perspiration from making love, and she loved the feel of their skin one against the other.

When Torac rolled from over her, he brought Leana with him so that her head was on his chest.

Both were silent, the pelting of the rain outside almost drowning out the heavy breathing. Unsure if he felt the same way, Leana was hesitant to speak, not wanting to break the spell they'd spun of a future of stolen kisses and wonderful lovemaking.

It was hours later that she woke. Torac remained asleep, his handsome features relaxed. She studied the slant of his eyebrows over long-lashed eyes. The sharp edge of his lightly bearded jaw and the lips that had brought so many sensations the night before.

When he took a deep breath and yawned, she waited for his gaze to meet hers. It was a few moments longer that she was able to continue committing him to memory as he seemed to be slow to wake.

"What are ye thinking?" His voice was gruff from sleep.

"That ye are quite handsome." Leana decided to be honest. "And that ye sleep quite soundly."

He chuckled. "It is ye who sleeps soundly. I got up a pair of times. Once to check on my steed and once because I thought to have heard something outside."

Leana was instantly awake. "A person?"

"It was a wee beast that took shelter under the roof."

Her body settled. "Ye will return to the guard post then?"

Turning to her, he brought Leana against him and pressed a kiss to her temple. Immediately she was aware that he was aroused, his hardness pressing into her stomach. The knowledge signaled to her body as it came to life.

"Torac," Leana whispered, praying that he read her mind and that she did not have to ask for him to make love to her again.

When his hands slid down her back to cup her bottom and lift her so that they could join, Leana almost cried with relief.

Torac rolled onto his back and lowered her onto his staff. Impaled on him, she held tightly onto his shoulders. With remarkable strength, Torac was able to guide her up and down as if she weighed no more than a feather. Soon, she didn't require guidance. She rested her knees on both sides of his hips and rode him.

Torac watched her intently through half-closed eyes as she raised and lowered over him again and again. Lips parted, he caressed her breasts. Then closing his eyes he threw his head back, grabbed her hips, and increased the pace.

Crying out, when the hard release sent the room spinning, Leana lost control. When she fell over him, Torac held her hips and continued driving into her until a few moments later, he too became lost to their passion.

"Come here," Torac took her arm and turned her to him. They'd broken their fast with awkward conversation. At least for her it felt that way. Unsure of what to say, what to think, and what to do, her mind whirled in every direction.

"What is wrong?" His gaze bore into hers. "Leana, we made love. I will claim ye as mine."

"Claim?" She turned away. "As a lover?"

Torac's eyebrows knit together. "As my woman. What else can I do? Ye are married. If ye were not, I would like to marry ye."

Even after he was gone away, Gawyn continued to ruin things. Leana sighed. "It may be better to leave it as it is. My father will never agree to it."

At the sound of his exasperated breath, Leana wanted to cry. She went to him and leaned against his chest. Finally, he wrapped his arms around her.

"Understand," she began. "I am not sure what to do. I do not know where he is or if he is alive."

His body stiffened. "And if he is dead?"

Leana shrugged. "How can we prove it?" She glanced toward the ground as if in deep thought. Torac waited to see what she would say.

Finally after a long moment she looked up and studied him then hesitantly she asked, "How do I know ye will not change? That ye will not beat me or mistreat me? Men change. Can be cruel."

The muscle on the side of his face flexed, but he managed a calm tone. "Must I remind ye daily that I am not him? I have never mistreated a woman or a child. I like the company of elders and enjoy animals. Other than my word, Leana, there is nothing else I can give ye."

After a moment's pause, he continued, "If ye wish, I can speak to yer father—"

"No," Leana interrupted. "Give me time. I ask that ye be patient, please."

Perhaps it was the stupidest thing she'd ever done, to ask

someone like Torac to wait for her. To give her time. He was so handsome, so desirable, that he could have any woman. That he chose her was surprising. If he also agreed to wait, she would be shocked.

With his fingers under her chin, Torac lifted Leana's face. "Ye are worth waiting for. I will return in a sennight. Not to pressure ye, but to spend time with ye."

At his words, her heart took flight and a tear slipped down her cheek. It was a moment she'd never forget. Not only did the man wish to be with her, but he seemed to accept the conditions she'd asked for.

"Be at ease and do not cry," Torac said pressing a kiss on her lips. "I understand."

AS THEY WALKED out to the stable, so that Torac could help her hitch the mare to the wagon, Torac gave her a questioning look. "I will keep watch to ensure ye are safe. We still do not know where the men are who burned the farmer's house.

Leana nodded. "I hope they are caught. It is horrible."

They went into the stable and he closed the distance between them. "As much as I enjoyed last night. It is much too dangerous for ye to be here alone. Ye should have gone with yer Da."

"I would have missed seeing ye." She smiled. "Not only that, but ye would have probably broken down the front door."

When he smiled, her heart flipped. "True. I would have been worried something happened."

Just before lifting her to the bench, Torac brought Leana against him one last time and kissed her until she lost her breath.

Leana held him for a few moments, eyes closed inhaling his scent. "It will be a long sennight."

CHAPTER NINE

"WORD HAS COME from the laird," Erik said by way of greeting the morning after Torac returned to the guard post. "We are to split in half. Warriors are required in Taernsby."

"Are the aggressors back?" Torac asked as he walked to where food was being prepared. "Who is going?"

As leader of the guard, it was ultimately Erik's decision. However, Torac was second-in-command and could decide whether to stay or go.

"We are one man down," Struan said joining them, "so I say we only send nine." The archer took Torac in for a moment, his eyes narrowing. "Ye look different."

Although he did his best to school his expression, Struan's narrowed eyes said he'd noticed Torac's look of surprise before he managed it. The archer was as keen with insight as he was clear with eyesight.

"I am sure Balgair will return to the keep. He can work on the wall," Erik stated matter-of-factly. The tone, however, was betrayed by the creases of worry around his mouth. "How does he fair?" His icy blue gaze met Torac's.

"Moving about a bit."

As they ate, it was decided to give the warriors a choice of whether they wished to go to Taernsby or remain at the guard post. Men fought better when having some sort of control over their lives.

Lined up in two rows, the warriors formed an impressive group. Even Graeme, the healer was large and well-built.

Auley, the cook, his young helper, along with the family who'd come to help out when there were more warriors at the guard post stood to the side waiting to hear what news would be shared.

Erik lowered his shoulders. "Nine of ye will go to Taernsby. There is a threat to the village and our laird has asked for more warriors there. I will take volunteers. Those that wish to remain here, can do so."

"What about us?" asked the man whose family came to work there.

"Ye will go to Taernsby as well," Torac stated. At the news that he would continue to work for the laird, the man nodded eagerly. "Thank ye."

"Step forward if ye wish to go."

Five men stepped forward. The others murmured amongst themselves, whether to go or not.

"I will go," Struan stated and looked to his archers. "Broden, Aran, do ye wish to go with me?"

At once the archers stepped forward.

Erik looked to Torac. "Ye will stay?"

"I wish to remain." Torac thought of Leana and the promise he'd made her. When Struan's lips inched up just a bit at the corners, it was hard not to kick him.

"I will go." One last man stepped forward.

The men who would leave were told to prepare for the following day.

"Who is she?" Struan said walking alongside as Torac went to see about his horse. "I bet it is the MacKern lass. She is lovely. But…"

"But what?" Torac all but growled.

"Married. Is she not?" Struan was no longer joking. "Guard yer heart my friend. Her husband may return."

Torac looked around to ensure no one overheard. "He will never return."

At the statement, Struan gave him a quizzical look. "Why are ye so sure?"

"I killed him."

Struan coughed, his eyes wide. "On the way back from seeing about Balgair? Where did ye put him?"

"No. It was months ago. When we came across that group of bandits. Remember, the ones who attacked the farmer and his family?"

"Oh. Aye." Struan nodded. "Does she know?"

After a long breath, Torac shook his head. "Not yet. I am not sure how to tell her."

"Is she mourning his loss? If so, ye may not have a chance at her heart."

A warrior walked into the stables. Torac motioned for Struan to follow him out to the back area and out of earshot. "She does not mourn him. Hopes that he will never return."

"So then she will be glad that ye cut him down."

"Or she will lose trust and reject me."

"There is that," Struan stated. "Which is why I have kept my heart guarded. Women are too fickle. Hard to understand. Never know how they will react. One moment they love ye, the next they stab ye."

Although he doubted sweet Leana would stab him, he wasn't as sure if she would feel at ease after he'd kept the truth from her. "I do not think she would stab me."

Needing to keep his mind busy, Torac volunteered to go on patrol. He and the young warrior, called Caelan, would ride as far as the western shore and back.

"Ye did not volunteer to go," Torac stated.

The young man shrugged. "I like it here."

"Would ye not like to get battle experience?"

The cold wind became harder as they rode west. Torac was glad to have brought his heavier cloak. The sky was gray, but it didn't seem to him to bring rain.

"Do ye not think there will be time for fighting if I remain?" Caelan asked. "I have fought already and although I do wish to defend our people, I also wish to remain alive."

Torac laughed. "I do as well."

As they continued forth, there was movement in the trees. Torac met Caelan's gaze and then looked to the woods. The young warrior nodded.

They slowed their steeds. "How many?" Torac asked.

"A pair of men on horses. They seem to be keeping an eye on us."

The village past the forest had been unfriendly to Clan Ross, up until recently. Although they'd come to an agreement and were on better terms, there had to be some that did not care for them at all.

Caelan untied the bow from the saddle and held it. Then he turned his horse toward the woods and stared in the direction of where the men were. He pulled an arrow from his quiver and set it.

"What do ye want?" he called out, his arrow at the ready.

Not replying, the men turned their steeds around and galloped away.

"Interesting," Torac said. "Idiots."

"Should we follow them?"

Torac shook his head. "Nay, they could have more with them. Best to continue forth for a bit and then turn around. I want to see if they reappear."

Once they arrived at the seashore, it had grown colder. The salty air greeted them along with an icy wind. As welcoming as the sounds of the waves were, the lack of sunlight removed any enticement to get closer.

They rode along the water's edge as gulls flew in circles, searching for a last meal before nightfall.

"I grew up near here," Caelan stated, looking out to the sea. "Every time I ride here, I am tempted to ride further, to where I grew up."

"Is it far?"

The young man shook his head. "No."

"So ye visit often?"

This time Caelan frowned and looked up to the sky. "Nay I do not. I am not welcome."

When he was not more forthcoming, Torac decided to drop the subject. "We should head back. Keep an eye out for our friends in the forest."

About an hour into the return the men in the forest appeared again. This time, they rode keeping pace with them.

"That is rather annoying," Caelan said. "Do ye think they need something?"

"If so they would have made it clear. I think they are wanting to see where we go."

They continued on at a faster pace. Having to travel along the trees, the men were left behind.

It was possible it was the same group that had attacked the farmers' homes. He would have to alert others and go in search and find out. Since it was just him and Caelan, going after them at the moment would be too dangerous.

Upon arriving at the guard post, Torac immediately assembled with more warriors, and they rode back to where they'd seen the men.

They searched until sundown, at that point it became hard to see, so they returned to the camp.

"Who do ye think they were?" Erik asked as they ate last meal.

"I have a feeling they were the same group who attacked the farmers and injured Balgair," Torac replied. "Not sure why."

Struan shook his head. "They are far from where they normally cause trouble."

"Perhaps headed to the village south of here," Erik said.

Could it be that they knew he'd been the one who'd killed Gawyn Smith? Torac figured it was doubtful as he himself hadn't been sure until recently. It was possible they wished to catch him alone.

In the morning he would go and search again. Unless they rode back north during the night, they would find them.

Two days later.

"I AM GOING to see about Balgair," Torac announced. He and

several warriors had searched the woods for past two days for the men who'd followed him and Caelan. Other than a doused campfire, they'd found no trace of them.

Struan and the warriors had left, which meant the ones left behind would remain and take turns patrolling. It would be an easy assignment. Three patrolling from the south up to the northeast portion of the region, three to the northwest, and three remaining at the camp. They would rotate posts so that one group would remain at camp every two days and rest.

"Take yer men with ye," Erik ordered. "From now on, we always travel in groups of three."

Torac wanted to argue. If he went to see Leana, he'd have to do so with two in tow.

Letting out a breath, he considered that if his men asked to go see someone alone, he would not allow it. If one of his men wanted to visit a woman, he'd go and wait outside for the man to do what he had to.

Along with Caelan, another warrior called Lachland mounted and prepared for the two-day trip that would include the village of Welland and passing near Leana's farm.

From the start, it was obvious his companions did not like each other. They replied to each other when necessary with grunts and kept their distance when dismounting.

Nearing Caelan, Torac glanced to where Lachland leaned on a tree keeping watch on his steed. The horses drank from a creek and then meandered to nibble on green grasses.

"Not friends?" Torac met Caelan's gaze.

The young warrior slid a look toward where Lachland stood. "Not friends."

"Ye will fight together. I do not care if ye hate one another."

"My oath as a warrior is to defend Clan Ross. He is part of it."

Satisfied with the response, Torac went to Lachland, who straightened at his nearing.

"Are we to leave?" he asked.

"Aye," Torac said. He stopped the warrior from stepping away. "As I just told Caelan. I do not care that ye do not like each other. Ye will fight together and we defend one another."

Lachland nodded. "I will never waiver when it comes to battle. To defend our people."

"Very well," Torac said. "Let us mount," he called out.

It was a few hours before they arrived in Welland. Athol, the constable, as usual, sat at a table outside the pub. He waved upon seeing them.

"'Tis good to see ye," he said in greeting. "I require yer help."

As they listened to the constable describe an argument between men who lived nearby, they were given food and ale by the tavern owner.

The day, although cool, was sunny and children took advantage to play. Running in circles while parents tended to their stands or shopped while keeping an eye out.

"Have ye seen Balgair?" Torac asked as he wished to know what to expect.

Athol nodded. "Aye, I stopped by there just the other day to see about him. He is recovering somewhat. Still in great pain when moving, but he and the hounds make slow treks out."

At the news, Torac was relieved. "I am going to see him."

"Oy! Lars." The constable called a lad over. "Go by Swan-noc's and tell her warriors are coming to visit."

The man gave Torac a knowing look. "'Tis best to warn her so she puts the devil hounds away."

"Aye, they are quite protective," Torac agreed.

After sending Caelan and Lachland to visit the arguing men, Torac decided to walk to visit Balgair.

"Torac." The sound of Leana's voice made his stomach tighten. He turned to see her walking from the market with a basket laden with items.

He wanted to rush forward and pull her into his arms. She must have read the intention in his expression because she hesitated in her steps. "I am glad to see ye." Her lips curved into a shy smile.

"Why are ye in Aldness? Are ye here alone? Ye should not be about without escort."

"I came with Beth and one of her sons. She has a sister near here." She turned to where the woman, Beth, watched them from a fruit stand. "We are about to return home."

Torac nodded. "Can I come to visit tomorrow?"

Her face brightened. "I would like that very much."

"Unfortunately, I will have two men with me. I cannot stay very long."

"I understand," Leana replied, her expression not dimming. "I look forward to seeing ye."

He motioned for her to follow, and she did until reaching the edge of a building. Then he took her hand and pulled her out of her friend's line of sight.

At once, he brought her against him and kissed her soundly. The kiss was quick but long enough to bring him to arousal.

Leana turned to look around, her eyes wide. "Someone could have seen."

"I could not resist." He touched her hand. "I will see ye on the morrow."

Unable to keep from it, he pressed a kiss to her cheek and hurried away. Best to walk away than to cause a scene.

"Torac," she called out and when he turned, she smiled.

To keep that smile on her face would become his life's goal. Never to see her sad, worried, or frightened. How would she react once he admitted his part in Gawyn's disappearance?

He would not tell her yet. Instead, he'd find a way to get time alone with her and convince Leana he meant for a future with her. Then he'd inform her. Ensure she knew he'd not realized he may have been the one who killed Gawyn until recently.

CHAPTER TEN

THAT BALGAIR WOULD never fight again was a horrible truth that had yet to fully sink in. Each morning he woke expecting to be at the guard post only to realize that once again he was at Swannoc's home.

That he depended on a woman for everything was becoming more unbearable by the day. It should be the other way around. A man should be the one who protected, cared for, and ensured no harm came to a woman.

He'd leave as soon as he could mount. Go as far away from there as possible. Hide two things from her. His embarrassment at being so weak, and his growing attraction to her.

A woman like Swannoc, independent, beautiful, and kind deserved a man who was able to defend her at all costs. Not to mention keeping her satisfied in bed.

His teeth threatened to shatter when he gritted them in order not to moan when sitting up. Despite him arguing he was better, Swannoc refused to allow him to sleep in the front room, stating how it would slow his recovery to sleep on a cot.

As much as he argued against taking the bedchamber from her, he had to admit it would be impossible to sleep on a small cot and keep from hurting his injured side.

It was early afternoon and he'd fallen asleep while sitting in the warm sun fletching arrows. Once he was better healed, he'd begin practicing with a bow and arrow. As his right side was stronger, Balgair expected it would be easier to shoot arrows than attempt to lift a sword or any other weapon.

He straightened and tentatively touched the area and was glad that it didn't hurt as much. The area remained tender, but he was able to walk and do more each day.

Later that day it would be time to change the dressing and see the progress of his wound.

Still unable to lift that arm, he'd donned a tunic that had been torn down the front and belted. Unable to put his boots on by himself, instead, he walked out wearing the knitted stockings Swannoc had made for him.

If any of the warriors saw him, they would laugh at the sight of him in a wrapped tunic and knitted socks.

It was quiet inside the house, and he expected Swannoc, and the dogs had gone into the village. A few sniffs of the air told him she'd not cooked before leaving. Balgair held a cane he'd made and used it to stand.

"There ye are." Torac appeared at the doorway. The male's gaze swept over him, but to his credit, his face remained passive. "It is good to see ye on yer feet."

Balgair motioned for his friend to come out to the small courtyard. "Come sit. Tell me what happens at the camp."

"I brought ye food. I saw Swannoc just before heading this way and she said ye would be hungry."

Taking the meat pies wrapped in cloth, Balgair nodded. "I am."

He ate as Torac told him of men leaving and going to Taernsby and about the patrols, the men in the forest, and that they'd yet to find the men who attacked them. The entire time,

Balgair listened intently missing what had been his life for the last decade. He'd joined the laird's guard at eight and ten after leaving the farm in search of excitement.

Now at nine and twenty, he was maimed for the rest of his life. And yet, he didn't regret his choice.

At Torac's pause, Balgair realized he'd asked a question. "I will be able to be on my way soon," Balgair said. "I need to leave."

"Where?"

"I can return to my family's farm. I will nae be much help. Do not know what else I can do." In truth the more he thought about it, the less he knew what to do. A part of him wished that he'd been killed, and all choice taken.

A low moan escaped when he adjusted himself in the seat. "As ye know, I am cousin to the laird. I wonder if he would want me to seek permission to leave the guard."

Torac shrugged. "In all probability, aye."

"What of yer plans to fish all day?" Torac continued, in an effort to lighten the mood.

"Aye, there is that," Balgair replied. "I will go to the keep. Speak to the laird. Seek advice."

Torac frowned. "'Tis not about what others think ye should do. Ye remain strong and can do what ye wish. Think about that."

"I thought I knew what I wanted," Balgair replied, then turned to look over his shoulder. "Now I cannae figure anything out."

A look crossed Torac's expression. "I must tell ye something."

Balgair waited.

"I am considering leaving the guard."

"The MacKern lass?"

Torac let out a breath. "Does everyone know how I feel about her?"

"'Tis obvious," Balgair said unable to keep from chuckling. "What of her husband?"

"He is dead."

"And ye know this how?"

"I killed him."

The sound of a dog barking in the distance, along with the ringing of bells hanging around the necks of some passing goats were all that broke the silence as the two men continued sitting, each lost in their own thoughts.

"Does she know?" Balgair asked.

"Nay."

"Ye must tell her." Balgair paused in thought. "When did it happen?"

"Do you remember when we fought those men, the one with the burned scarred face?"

"Oh, aye." Balgair scratched his beard.

"Her husband was that man." A tortured expression marred Torac's face. "I do not know what her reaction will be."

"He and his comrades killed an innocent family. He more than deserved it."

Torac shook his head. "She is untrusting of men and thinks them to be deceitful. I should have told her as soon as I realized who he was."

The last thing Balgair could do at the moment was to give advice as he himself was confused about what to do. In his mind, he could return to his life's work. However, with each movement, his body contradicted the notion.

"I wish to leave. Can ye hire a wagon?"

With a look of doubt, Torac replied, "How long before ye are in too much pain to continue?" When Balgair didn't reply, he continued, "I can take ye to the keep. But it will have to be in a few days. I have to ensure someone can take over my duties. Can ye wait a sennight?"

Just then Swannoc returned, her hounds in tow. "I have to change yer bandages today."

Without meaning to, Balgair grimaced. It would be painful. Her gaze snapped to Torac. Yer men are out front.

"They can wait. I will remain to see how he fares."

At her signal, the dogs relaxed and settled for a nap in the afternoon sun. Torac went to fetch a bucket of water and Swannoc returned with bandages and her basket of tonics.

With graceful moves, she wrapped her braided hair into a bun at the nape of her neck. Then she donned an apron and waited for Torac's return.

"Ye are too weak to travel as yet. I do not mind if ye remain longer," her bright green eyes met his. "Please, wait."

If she only knew that the longer he remained, the harder it would be to leave. Did her eyes darken when she was in the throes of making love? Balgair tore his gaze away as his mind had wandered to a place he had no right to go.

Upon inspection, the wound was healing outwardly. However, Balgair could tell that it was the opposite inside his body.

By her pinched expression, Swannoc must have thought the same.

Once Torac returned with the water, she thanked him. The warrior left after Balgair was bandaged.

"I am healing," Balgair stated.

"It is the portion we do not see that takes longer to heal." Swannoc sat in the chair Torac had vacated. "What do ye plan to do upon leaving?"

Despite the fact he'd just had the conversation with Torac, Balgair's mind went blank. Perhaps it was the beautiful bewitching gaze that remained steady on his.

Swannoc smiled as if he'd said something interesting. "I believe that ye will struggle until making up yer mind. Once that is done, then all will be as it should."

Noticeably, she did not say, "all would be well." Neither knew if he would ever fully recover. Often in these last days, he'd wondered if perhaps he was dying.

"I've considered the seashore," he began. "I like the smell of salty air. I could fish."

Swannoc leaned back with a wistful expression on her pretty face. "I like the sea as well. I grew up on the eastern shore of Barra."

As she spoke, she told him of her childhood. Of her parents dying. Of both her and her brother getting married.

Swannoc had already told him that both her husband and wee son had drowned when the ship they were on sunk. He'd been among the people rescuing the fortunate few who had survived. However, their paths had not crossed.

"… he loved teasing me about my love of the sea." Her lips curved when speaking of her late husband making it obvious it had been a love match. "Little did we ever suspect it would take him and our son from me."

"It has been almost three years hence and I've finally settled. Loss makes it hard to find a new place in one's life." She turned to him. "I suppose what ye are going through is similar. Ye lost yer place in the life ye planned."

Not wanting her to be sad, he lightened the mood with a chuckle. "Not long ago, that day, the day of the attack, I told Torac, I considered leaving the guard."

Swannoc giggled. "I suppose the fates heard ye."

"Aye, they must have."

"Would ye go with me?" The words were out of his mouth before he could stop them. Balgair fought to keep a neutral expression, but he couldn't help searching her face for what her response would be.

Swannoc stood and leaned over him. "I may consider it." Then to his astonishment, she pressed a soft kiss to his lips. "I trust ye can see about emptying the bucket and getting fresh water." With that, she went into the house leaving him frozen in place.

Had she just said she would consider going with him? Balgair turned to ask, but she'd gone into the house.

Even if his side split in half, he would fetch the water and two more if she asked. Balgair's lips curved as he got to his feet. The hounds lifted their heads and followed his progress to the well. Neither felt the need to see about him, which told him he must have been walking with better balance.

Once Torac returned, he would go to the keep and gather the rest of his belongings, his coffer of coin, and return to propose marriage to Swannoc.

When he reached for the handle of the well, his side protested profusely, and he let out several breaths.

What the hell was he thinking? She'd probably said it out of pity. He hung his head and let out another breath.

"Balgair? Is something wrong?" Swannoc had come up without him knowing.

He met her gaze. "Ye are kind. It would not be fair for ye to be tied to a cripple. Thank ye for saying ye would go with me."

"I expected ye would think that." She cupped his jaw. "I wish to be with ye. Am anxious for ye to recover. I care very much for ye, Balgair."

With his right arm, he pulled her against him and kissed her in a way that left no doubt he wished to be with her as well.

CHAPTER ELEVEN

A SENNIGHT HAD passed and Torac had yet to appear. Despite reminding herself that she should have expected it, Leana couldn't help the ache that tightened in her chest each time she looked toward the road between the farms.

"Are ye expecting someone?" her father asked following her line of sight. He gave her a knowing look. "The warrior took a keen interest in ye. Did he not?"

Hoping her shrug helped to dissuade her father from asking more, Leana turned back to the table on which she cut up vegetables. "Whether he did or not, it matters little. Gawyn could return and have me thrown in prison for daring to look at another man."

"I wish ye had never married him." Her father's tone was hard. "I do not understand it."

In hindsight, it was hard for her to understand why she'd allowed the man into her life. "I made a stupid mistake."

Swallowing hard. It was time to tell her father the truth. That she never married Gawyn. She'd lied because he'd refused even after they'd lain together. "Da, I should tell ye that—"

"Someone comes." Her father craned his neck to look through the doorway. "Looks to be him."

"Who?" Wiping her hands on her apron, she went to her

father and peered out. At the sight of Torac and two others, her heart skipped. "Oh, dear."

Was it fate telling her it was time to tell them both the truth? That she'd never married Gawyn and that even if he did return, he had no hold over her. Her heart hammered as her father waved to the men from the doorway.

Torac's dark gaze went to her, holding it for a bit before he spoke. "We are returning through on our way back to the guard post. Can we take our rest here?"

"Of course. Of course." Her father grinned, delighted to have male company. Since the men who'd come to help with the harvest had left, it was only occasionally that he saw anyone. Beth's husband stopped by, but it was rare as he had plenty of work to take care of himself.

While the men rounded to the back of the house to wash up and put the horses in the corral, Leana hurriedly finished cutting the vegetables, grabbing a few more so there would be plenty of stew for everyone.

She'd already kneaded the dough for bread. Once she placed the vegetables into the boiling water along with cut pieces of lamb and a few herbs for flavor, she poured ale into cups.

"Do not go to trouble for us." Torac's deep voice washed over her like a warm blanket.

Leana whirled to find that they were alone, her father was outside with the other two warriors. Immediately she closed the distance between them and wrapped her arms around his waist. How she loved the feel of his hard body and when he hugged her in return, it was as if finding the place she'd been lost from.

"A quick kiss before we're seen," Torac murmured into her hair. Lifting her face to him, she closed her eyes just as his lips pressed to hers.

The kiss was hurried, passionate, and so very wonderful. His tongue probed her lips, and she parted them gladly, enjoying every second of it.

Abruptly, he pushed away and turned to the bowl holding the dough. "Do ye require any help?"

"Ye can help me take the ale out," she replied, still a bit disoriented by the kiss.

He slid a look to her and then to the doorway as her father peered in. "Ah, there ye are," he said with a smile. "Bring the ale, lass."

They walked out and Leana sat with them for a moment. It was a delightful way to spend the afternoon. Her father telling the two men who accompanied Torac about how the warriors had learned to harvest wheat. They laughed about some mishaps all the while she and Torac stole glances at each other.

Leana returned inside to bake the bread wondering if there would be time to speak to Torac and her father alone.

Time passed much too quickly. The men continued speaking with her father, the two young warriors asking questions about the area and farming, while Torac stood a bit away looking out towards the forest.

"Is something wrong?" Leana said. She carried a bucket of food for the pigs, and he took it from her. They walked toward the pen together.

"Someone is about there, past the berry bushes." Torac didn't look to the area, but Leana did. She didn't see anyone at first, but then a man's face appeared and glared at her. It was

Tom.

"I know who it is. Probably looking to see what happens."

"Who?" Torac asked.

"Gawyn's brother, Tom."

The large man must have realized he was seen because he came out of the woods and walked directly toward Torac. The other warriors immediately stood, their attention on Tom.

"She's with my brother," Tom said. "Ye should stay away from 'er."

"What do ye want Tom?" Leana said, her throat constricting at Tom's comment. Gawyn's family knew she and he never married.

Her father had managed the distance. "Leave her be. Go on now, Tom. 'Tis obvious ye've been drinking."

"She never married him ye know," Tom said lifting a jar to his mouth. "Allowed him between her legs. Not married."

The blood in her veins turned to ice and Leana felt it drain from her face. Why had the man decided to speak now?

Before anyone could react Torac's fist connected with Tom's jaw and the drunk man stumbled backward. Much too large to be knocked by one hit, he shook his head. When he grinned, his teeth were reddened with blood.

"Defending her virtue?" Tom shouted. "She has none. Admit it, Leana! Ye slept with me while with my brother."

"Liar!" Leana cried out, unable to believe what happened. Just as she was about to turn, Torac grabbed the drunken man by the tunic.

There was a loud *oof* when Torac's fist sunk into Tom's stomach. The man leaned over letting out a thunderous burp then threw up.

Tom began laughing, his face twisted with anger at the same time. "Ye are nae better. A coward, ye have not told anyone have ye. I could nae figure it out, but now I know."

He struggled for breath before continuing. "Aye, I know ye," he gasped out. "Ye are the man who killed 'im. Ye killed Gawyn."

In the stunned silence that followed, Tom stared at Torac. "Ye will get yers. I have men to fight with as well."

The drunk man groaned, then lifted the jar back to his lips. "Take heed. I will find ye." With that he turned and walked back into the woods, heading toward where he lived.

Seeming to know Torac, her father and Leana needed privacy, Torac's companions made the excuse of following Tom, to ensure the man left.

"Is it true?" her father asked, his eyes boring into Leana's. "Ye never married Gawyn?"

If ever there was a time she wished to be dead, this was one. The disappointment on her father's face shattered her heart into pieces.

"Aye." She looked to Torac. "He refused to. I said we were because I did not know what else to do. I am so sorry, Da."

Her father rubbed both hands down his face. "I do nae know what to say. What to think." He looked at Torac. "What about it? Did ye truly kill 'im?"

Torac swallowed. "I killed a man with a burned scarred face. He was with a group of men that killed a farmer and his family. We caught them and he fought. It could be it was him I killed, aye."

That Torac had never told her about it was astonishing. He'd allowed her to think for months that Gawyn could return. Kept the truth from her.

As much as she wished to ask questions, the moment was not hers. She'd been exposed for a whore.

Her father and Torac probably believed she'd given herself to Tom as well.

Unable to take the humiliation, sobs escaped, and Leana ran to the house, through the main room, and into her bedchamber, closing the door behind her.

There were so many warring emotions churning inside. Like a storm brewing, it was best to try to hold things at bay. Once Leana relinquished control, it would be unstoppable.

All strength dissipated and Leana sank into a chair balling her hands into fists. Letting out a long breath at realizing she'd held it, the room seemed to darken. Perhaps clouds had converged, or it was the fact there was little light in the room. Either way, she did not move from where she sat for many hours.

That night she crawled into bed, still without any outward show of emotion. Her father must have been as confused as she was because he did not knock on her door to ask that they speak.

She'd heard Torac and his men leave, the men's voices low as they'd thanked her father for the hospitality. How embarrassed her father must have been at what had been disclosed. Her chest tightened at the thought.

What would happen next?

"I UNDERSTAND," HER father said the next day as she hurried about the house cleaning the dishes from the day before and preparing a light first meal.

Her gaze lowered, as she couldn't bear to look her father in the eye, Leana nodded. "I do not know how to make things right. I have never lied to ye. Ye do not deserve the humiliation my actions caused ye yesterday."

"Lass, ye are not the first, nor will ye be the last, to live with a man without being married. 'Tis something that happens. Do not worry yerself over it."

Leana wiped away tears that slipped down her cheeks. "I hated lying to ye. I promise that I have never been with Tom."

"I did nae believe him that. I never thought ye to lie to me. Never do it again. Ye and I, we have only each other." When her father sniffed and blew his nose with a rag, she rushed to him and threw her arms around his shoulders.

"Please forgive me, Father."

Her father nodded. "What of ye and Torac? He believes he killed Gawyn?"

"It matters not. I am sure he will never return." Leana sniffed. "Why did he not tell anyone that Gawyn was dead? He could have saved us from so much."

They sat at the table and ate porridge and leftover toasted bread. Her father shook his head. "I wonder if he really did kill Gawyn."

"He seems to think he did. Did he say anything else about it?"

"No. We avoided any talk of Gawyn. He did say he would come and see about us in a few days."

How could she ever face him again?

THAT AFTERNOON, BETH and her son came over. The young man saw about ensuring the horses were brushed down and fed, and then would repair a portion of fencing.

Her father hobbled alongside, speaking to him of what else needed to be done.

"He seems to be moving about easier," Beth said watching Leana dig up potatoes.

Leana looked over her shoulder to where her father was. "Aye, I think his leg is almost healed."

"What is it?" Beth studied her. "Ye seem sad."

"Tom came yesterday, while the warrior Torac and two others stopped by here for a rest."

Beth's lips curved. "The man, Torac, is very handsome. He is attracted to ye."

"Aye, well after what happened, I may never see him again." She went on to tell her about Tom's inopportune visit and how he'd blurted not only that she'd never married Gawyn, but that she'd also been with him." She left out the part about Torac killing Gawyn as she wasn't sure how to absorb it yet.

Her friend let out a hearty laugh. "No one would ever lay with that smelly oaf. I am sure he did not believe it."

"I have no idea. I ran into the house. It was so humiliating."

"How did yer Da react?" Beth had been privy to the truth as Leana had to tell someone about not being married to Gawyn. They'd tried to come up with a way for Gawyn to marry her but had failed.

"He is hurt but has forgiven me."

"Well, 'tis a good thing he knows. If that idiot is not dead and ever returns ye will not have to allow him here."

Leana sat back on her legs. "Father was so understanding. This morning I apologized for lying to him. That is what hurt him, that I was untruthful." She wiped away an errant tear. "I feel relief that he knows the truth. I suppose that is one thing I can thank the stinky oaf for."

"I do not understand why that family continues to torture ye over it. It is obvious neither ye nor yer father knows where Gawyn is."

Leana looked to Beth. "If Tom claims Torac killed Gawyn, why have he and Willa been torturing us about it?"

A look of surprise took over Beth's face. "I wonder if Tom remembers what he blurted out while drunk about what happened to Gawyn. Because if Torac killed Gawyn, it must have been because they were up to no good. Now he has admitted to being part of a group of robbers."

Leana let out a long breath. "What will happen now?"

"Let us talk of other more pleasant things," Beth said.

They spoke of the upcoming colder weather and what to do to prepare for it. Leana was grateful for Beth's company as it took her mind away from Torac and wondering if he would ever return.

And if he did, would she forgive him for not speaking out?

CHAPTER TWELVE

THE WIND SO cold it seeped straight into their bones. When the weather was this cold, people tended to stay close to home, which meant less trouble. Erik had decided they would not patrol that day, for it Torac was grateful.

Now that there were fewer of them, they ate inside the main building. Two tables had been set up along with a sideboard that held dishes and such.

Auley and the lad served them crisp pork with potatoes and bread, a hearty delicious meal. Torac noticed that Caelan and Lachland sat at different tables. Whatever had occurred between the two of them seemed to be serious.

Although it wasn't usually anything to be worried about, Torac would keep an eye on them. If they were outwardly hostile toward the other, one of them would have to be sent to another location.

"What is it?" Struan asked as he sat next to him. He'd returned to spend a pair of days with the archers.

"Keeping an eye on two men. They seem to hate one another."

"Who?

"Lachland, he's one of yers. And Caelan, one of mine." Torac let out a sigh. "Although archers and warriors rarely get along, these two seem to detest each other."

Struan's gaze moved from Caelan to Lachland. "I think to know why, but I will tell ye about it later."

TORAC GAWKED AT the other warrior. "Are ye sure?"

"I am, saw them once," Struan replied. "It was sundown, and I went to relieve myself over there,"—he pointed to the area behind the cottage—"heard noises and peered through the trees. Caelan was bent at the waist, while Lachland fucked him from behind."

Unsure what to think, Torac's eyes widened. "If that happened, then why the animosity?"

His friend shrugged. "It could be one of them does not wish to admit their attraction to men. 'Tis not our concern."

"It is my concern if they are to fight with me." Torac looked in the direction of where the archers practiced. "I do not care who fucks who. But..."

"They are good men. I have no worries that their lack of caring for one another affects how they fight." Struan lifted his bow and quiver. "Let me show them who is the best." He strolled away, his fur cape around his wide shoulders.

Frowning, Torac looked to where the warriors fought. Lachland was holding his own against a larger man. He had to admit, the man was good—remarkable even. When on the battlefield he trusted him.

Looking to Caelan, he recalled his statement of not being welcome at his home. Was it because of his inclination for men? A shame really, it wasn't as if he or any person would ever have a chat with one's parents about it.

Perhaps, like Struan, someone in the family had caught him with another man.

Although Torac didn't understand why some were attracted to their same gender, neither did he worry overmuch about it. Some men given a warm male body after months of not being with a woman would not hesitate. However, neither would they admit to it.

"When do ye go and take Balgair to see the laird?" Erik asked, following his line of sight. "What is he going to do?"

Torac shrugged. "I am not sure. I do not think he will work on the wall. He will either return to his family or the seashore."

"I believe his family lives on the coast of Skye," Erik said. "It could be our fate. Like him to be injured in battle and unable to fight again."

Since Balgair's injury, he and others had discussed the subject. Torac wondered about Erik, now that the man was married, he had to consider himself and the bairns that would come.

"I have been considering leaving the guard." He wasn't sure why he'd blurted it out. He'd told Balgair, but to say it to the leader was something totally different.

Erik stared at him as if he'd grown a second head. "Ye? Leave? I never expected to hear those words from such a good warrior. It is yer life."

"Aye, I know. However, I am almost five and thirty. Getting too old to continue." Torac watched the much younger and stronger men at practice. "I am the eldest man here."

"When?" Erik's jawline tensed. "I do not wish to lose ye. Ye and I have fought and been together for ten years at least."

"Aye, we have." Torac smiled. "Yer like the son I never had."

"I am but three years younger," Eric stated rolling his eyes.

"Why now?"

Torac shrugged and lifted his sword. "I have not made my mind up yet. Practice?"

They sparred, both not exactly putting much effort into it.

"I want to do something enjoyable before I die," Torac said thrusting forward. "Not sure what."

"Ye can do that here." Erik swung and he blocked. "Go fishing. Whoring. Do not leave."

Torac sliced across and Erik successfully evaded. "I do not want to fish. Women, that is not a bad idea." In truth, he had not thought of bedding anyone since Leana. She was the woman he wanted more than anything.

"Then ye have no plan," Erik stated, making Torac realize that indeed he did not. Yet the restlessness that stirred would not abate. It was constant.

Erik lowered his sword and walked forward. It wasn't until his chest touched the tip of Torac's sword that he realized he was lost in thought.

His friend's face brightened. "Ye are in love."

"What? No," Torac said replacing his sword into its scabbard. "I am not."

"Aye, ye are. I heard rumors about ye and the beautiful Leana. The shy lass. What happened?"

"Balgair and I are about the same age and just before he was injured we talked about what we'd do when no longer able to fight. Neither of us finds the idea of working on the wall to our liking. I have thought about it since then."

Erik mulled over Torac's statement, his icy gaze moving across the land before them. "Once I became a warrior, I never planned for a future. 'Tis better not to, in my opinion. Now that I am with Esme, I believe it makes me a better fighter. I have a desperate desire to live and return to her."

Considering the man had been a warrior all his life and never shirked from duties, Torac was not astounded at the words. Simply because when they'd fought since Erik had married, the warrior had not changed at all when it came to his aggression toward the enemy.

A part of him feared that if he were to settle with a woman, he'd lose his strength of mind on the battlefield. Never would he want to be a hindrance to others, and not be the support necessary when fighting.

"I had not thought of how a woman makes for a stronger warrior," Torac admitted, his gaze going past Erik. "It may all be for naught."

Erik frowned. "Why?"

"I killed the man she lived with. It was months ago, and she did not care for him. But she may find it a reason not to trust me."

His friend nodded in understanding. "Give her time."

"I wonder if I would be a better fighter with a wife," Torac said more to himself.

"Not everyone is. Some men do have to leave the battle-field. If ye are terrified of leaving a widow and orphaned bairns, ye will be of no use as a warrior." Erik's tone was firm.

"Riders come!" a warrior called out and they went to stand with the others to see who came.

It was Gavin, a warrior from Taernsby. He dismounted and allowed someone to take his steed. "I will stay until the morrow. My mount requires rest."

"How are things?" Torac asked genuinely concerned.

"Not good," Gavin admitted. "We believe the same ones who came before, have returned. A group of about thirty. They have a ship moored out by the small isle off the coast."

Erik grunted. "Who are they? What do they want?"

Attackers had come a few months earlier, they'd been driven away. Now, however, they had to be aware of the size of the Ross army. Whoever they were, had no chance of ever beating them.

"If they wish to settle here, they are approaching it the wrong way," Torac added.

"Aye," Gavin replied. "I do not believe they wish to settle. They are in all probability Norse with no plan but to pillage small villages and escape before we can catch them."

He went on to inform them that Laird Ross was sending birlinns with warriors and that they were to keep guard on the surrounding villages.

"Since Welland and Aldness are not in an area that is in danger, he has asked that ye guard the farms just north of Taernsby."

Erik blew out a breath. "I will leave Torac and Lachland behind. The rest of us go with ye in the morning."

Eight additional men would make a difference, but in Torac's opinion, the laird should be sending guardsmen from the north. Since he'd not been at the keep for some time, he wasn't aware of any problems. It could be the isle was under siege there too.

"Have ye heard of any problems near the keep?"

Gavin nodded. "Aye, there is a problem the Ross brothers are handling with their men. Seems the Uisdein is causing problems, so the guards are trying to keep the peace."

The men went to prepare the belongings they would take. Auley and his helper began loading their wagon as they would be going to the field with the men. Torac and Lachland would have to fend for food themselves.

"I promised Balgair to take him to the keep, but it will have to wait," Torac informed Erik.

THE NEXT MORNING the men ate leftover stew that Auley reheated, with bread and apples. Torac helped bring buckets of water to wash out the huge pot while the men loaded their horses and mounted.

Once done, he placed the pot onto the back of the wagon.

"Ensure the hounds are fed," Auley said patting the dog that had been there since they'd arrived. The dog hopped onto the back of the wagon, while two new ones that had discovered Auley's willingness to feed them would remain.

The dogs attempted to follow the wagon until Torac whistled and called them back.

Erik arrived from the direction of his home and looked to Torac. "Take time to decide what ye wish to do. Talk with her." With that, he rode off to catch up with the other warriors.

Inside the guardhouse, Lachland sharpened his sword with a stone, his face stoic. When he looked to Torac, his expression was angry. "Why did he decide I should remain behind?"

"It has nothing to do with yer ability as a warrior."

THEY MOUNTED IN order to head to Aldness, where Torac planned to ask the constable's son to come and care for the livestock and keep watch while he and Lachland patrolled.

It was a few hours later that they met with the lad, who eagerly accepted after reiterating that he hoped to serve the laird as guard one day.

Once the lad headed to the guard post, with hastily packed clothes, a sword, and bundles of food his mother insisted he take, Torac decided he should see about Balgair.

"Where will we sleep tonight?" Lachland asked. The man was young still, perhaps barely twenty, but he was a good warrior and a steadfast member of the guard. Obviously, Erik left him behind to separate him from Caelan.

"We will see."

Upon first seeing him, Balgair seemed to be much better. He met them at the door and was understanding of why Torac could not go to the keep.

"I will hire a wagon and go. There is no need for ye to worry about it," the warrior said when they sat down and were offered a meal. They ate a delicious meal of roasted pig and vegetables, washing it down with ale.

Lachland burped loudly. "I need to find a wife that cooks as good as ye fair Swannoc."

The green-eyed beauty smiled at Lachland. "I am sure ye can if ye set yer mind to it."

Although Lachland's comment took Torac by surprise after what Struan had witnessed, he decided not to give it much thought. It could be that Lachland had relations with both men and women. Not his business.

"Ye can stay here tonight if ye wish," Swannoc said, sliding a look to Balgair, whose lips curved. "I will stay in the room with Balgair."

"Thank ye," Lachland replied. "We'd planned to sleep outdoors. But it is getting quite cold at night."

A bark of laughter escaped from Torac. "I planned to rent a room at the tavern. Ye could have slept outdoors if ye wished."

Balgair joined in with a chuckle. "Torac will do what he can to not sleep outside. He will lay with the ugliest wench just to have a roof overhead."

"Have ye heard of any more problems with the group that torched the farmer's home?" Torac asked both Balgair and Swannoc.

"Nay," Swannoc replied. "They are probably hiding since they know ye and yer men are after them."

A thought occurred. "Balgair, can ye inform our laird about it? He may wish to send a contingency here so that we can search better for them."

"Where are ye going on the morrow?" Balgair asked, with a soft curve to the corners of his lips.

Torac considered his reply. "To finish our patrol of the lands."

CHAPTER THIRTEEN

WHEN WILLA AND Tom appeared, Leana tensed. She stood near the stables and hopefully out of her father's earshot.

"It is true?" Willa said without preamble. "That guard killed Gawyn?"

When Leana didn't reply, she stomped closer. "Well?"

Confused as to what happened, Leana narrowed her gaze at Tom. "Ask yer brother, he is the one that told us."

"I did not," Tom lied. "The man confessed to ye, and I overheard."

"Liar," Leana snapped. "Leave me be. Believe what ye want?"

Willa glared. "Why did he confess to killing him? Was it because ye asked 'im to?"

"No," Leana replied. "It was Tom that accused Torac of killing Gawyn. I did not expect Gawyn to be dead."

"That makes little sense," Willa said looking to Tom, who shrugged as if he too were confused.

They were a family of idiots that Leana had been cursed to live near. In all probability, Tom had gone home and fabricated lies to keep from admitting he'd known all along Gawyn was dead. If he had then he'd be forced to admit to being a thief and a murderer.

"I do not care what ye believe. I want nothing to do with the lot of ye." Leana started to round them, but Tom grabbed her arm. "Ye are a lying bitch."

When his fist sunk into her stomach, Leana fell forward unable to catch her breath.

"If I find out ye told that man to kill Gawyn, I will kill ye meself," Tom said looking down at her with an evil smile.

"I-I d-did not know any of th-the guards before they came," Leana managed breathlessly. "Why would the man say to have k-illed Gawyn?"

Willa grabbed Leana's hair and lifted her head from the ground. "The truth will come out. Whore."

"If that warrior returns. We will sort him out," Tom said. "My friends and I."

They hurried away at hearing her father calling out for her. Leana sat up and blew out a breath. She was sure he'd notice she'd been hurt and feel guilty about it.

"Da. I am here," Leana called out, standing. "Had a fall."

Her father hurried over as fast as he could, using his cane to help him remain stable. "What happened?" His face was etched with worry as he took her arm. "Did ye faint? Ye're pale."

"I am fine. Just a bit light-headed. Nothing to worry about." She smiled at him. "Ye have a clumsy daughter."

She managed a smile and wiped dirt from her skirts as her stomach protested the movements. Something had to be done.

"Da, I need to take the wagon to town tomorrow. Can ye help me hitch the mare to it in the morning?"

Her father studied her. "Why? Ye just went a couple of days ago."

She'd vowed not to lie to him and here she was about to do it. "I have to see about some herbs the constable's wife promised me. Also, I want to speak to him about what Tom admitted about Gawyn being dead."

"I will go with ye then." Her father gave her a stern look. "I do not know why I had not thought about it."

"He was drunk. What if he denies it?" Leana hoped to dissuade her father. "It may be best not to say anything."

Finally unable to dissuade her father from going, Leana was forced to go to Welland with her father.

When speaking to the constable, they were glad to hear that he was interested in what they stated. He promised to speak to Torac about it and to visit them once everything was settled.

Despite her wish to confront Torac, the best outcome was to let the men in authority take over. In due course, she would speak to Torac and ask for an explanation as to why he did not tell her he'd killed Gawyn.

If it was true, it meant that Torac was no different than other men. He'd kept the secret while courting her. He'd lied. There was no other way of seeing it.

Torac was just as untrustworthy as Gawyn had been. Perhaps not so cruel, or a thief, but then again, there was no way to know what he was truly capable of.

"Why are ye so glum?" her father asked. "It seems all will be cleared up. That viper Willa will have no reason to continue to confront ye."

"True," Leana said letting out a breath. "I am glad for it."

"Something else is wrong. Does it have to do with the warrior, Torac?" Her father turned away, his eyes on the road ahead. "Ye are wondering about him?"

"Of course I am," Leana cried out, her voice sounding shrill. "He lied to us Da. He allowed the Smiths to torture and blame us for Gawyn's disappearance."

Her father sighed. "He may not have known—"

"I no longer trust him and never wish to see him again." Leana crossed her arms. "I only trust one man. Ye."

"People often lie for reasons we do not know. Ye yerself felt the need to do so."

Her father's words rang true and yet, Leana could not dispel the disappointment she felt.

They rode in silence until reaching the Mackinnon's farm.

"I must speak to Calum," her father said referring to Beth's husband. They stopped and her father was helped down by Beth's son.

She couldn't help but to chuckle knowing her father made up the excuse to visit and tell his friend about what had occurred at the village with the constable.

"I did nae expect to see ye today," Beth said with a bright smile when Leana walked into the kitchen.

"Aye, we come from Welland. Da wanted to stop and talk with yer Calum." She sat down accepting a cup of cider. "I have news."

"What happened?" Immediately Beth sat opposite her, leaning forward. "Tell me."

Leana told her about Torac killing Gawyn and about Tom and Willa's visit that day. "We went to speak to the constable. He is going to talk to Torac."

"He killed Gawyn?" Beth's wide-eyed gaze took her in. "That is news indeed."

"Aye, in a way I feel better knowing Gawyn will never return." Leana closed her eyes. "Beth, Torac lied to me. Never said anything until Tom spewed it out when drunk."

Love for her friend grew when Beth became indignant. "He should have said something. Why would he not?"

"I can nae figure it out," Leana said. Then reconsidered. "Aye, I can. He asked to court me and probably thought I would nae wish to be with the man who killed my husband."

Beth shook her head. "I suppose it is understandable." When Leana opened her mouth to rebuke the statement, Beth held up a hand. "Nothing excuses that he allowed ye to be mistreated because of a lie. However, ye did say, he thought he may have killed Gawyn, but he is nae sure."

"Let us speak of something else," Leana said looking around the tidy house. "Winter will be approaching. We need to ensure to have warm blankets. Should we work together to spin wool to make them?"

They continue talking and planning for getting together in the next days. Both Calum and Beth insisted they remain for last meal, which they did.

It was dark when they returned home, but it didn't mean they could rest.

Once her father put the horse in the stable, he began noticeably limping.

"Go inside Da and start the fire in the hearth," Leana said. "I will ensure the animals are fed. Then I will join ye."

When he didn't protest, Leana was glad to have suggested it. He was probably overly tired and in pain. Put herbs in the kettle," she called after him.

Leana made quick work of feeding the goats and the pigs.

The chickens were less interested as they were already in the coop for the night.

At the sight of a beautiful bright full moon, Leana stopped and looked up at the starry sky. It was breathtakingly beautiful.

Suddenly, she was yanked backward, a calloused hand clasped over her mouth, and despite her struggles she was dragged into the forest.

CHAPTER FOURTEEN

FOR AN UNEXPLAINABLE reason, Torac woke in a foul mood. He sat up from the cot and looked around Swannoc's home. He supposed it was Balgair's now as well.

Too restless to stay in bed, he got up and dressed. Moments later, he woke Lachland. "We should go."

"We have not broken our fast," Lachland grumbled.

"Get up."

It was obvious Lachland was not happy to be woken early but was too good a warrior to grumble. Instead, he dressed and looked to Torac. "Where to?"

"The village square then we ride back towards the camp. And I have to stop at the MacKern farm."

By the time they mounted and rode to the village square some people mingled about starting their day. Thankfully a woman was selling food outside her house. They purchased the flavorful flatbread and meat to break their fast. No one else was about, the constable was probably still abed, so they left.

As they rode toward where Leana lived, his chest tightened with a sick feeling. In his gut, Torac expected something was wrong. He searched the horizon for smoke, telling him there was a fire, but it was clear. Then he looked toward Welland, the road was empty except for a lone man on a wagon heading toward them at a quick pace.

Soon they caught up with the man signaled them to stop. "Warriors. Are ye joining the search?"

"What search?" Torac asked, his gaze moving past the man to where three men on horseback appeared, galloping toward them.

"The MacKern lass was taken. Her da, Eli, has been searching for her all night."

At the words, it was as if a fist sunk into his stomach and Torac gasped in air. "What happened?"

The man did not have any information, other than to tell them Leana had gone missing the night before. Then men on horseback arrived, they were headed to the MacKern's to tell Eli they'd not found Leana anywhere in the area surrounding the village.

Torac urged his horse to a gallop with Lachland close behind. He jumped off at reaching Leana's home and raced into the house.

Hunched over the table, Eli held his head, jerking up at the door opening. Upon seeing Torac, he tried to stand but failed. He'd obviously reinjured his leg. "Leana. Leana is gone," he sputtered, his face crumbling. "My beautiful lass is gone." The man began to cry, a pitiful sight of anguish so deep, Torac has to clear his throat.

"Did ye see who took her?"

"Nay," Eli said wiping his face with his sleeve. "She went out to feed the goats...and pigs...she never...never returned."

The man's reddened eyes met his. "I fell asleep. But woke with a start. It was late and I realized not to have heard her return. It was when I realized she was gone. I searched the farm with a torch, then hitched the horse and searched more."

Eli had gone across to the Mackinnon's who'd joined in the search, and it was the son who'd gone to Welland to alert the constable.

There was much to do. With only him and Lachland left, there weren't any men at that time to do a complete search. Torac would have to rely on the men from the village and local farmers who could help.

Moments later, Calum Mackinnon entered and informed Eli that he'd recruited several more men to help.

Torac went out with Calum, after assisting Eli to a chair outside the door so he could hear what was said.

With a stick, Calum drew a crude map of the area. There were eight men who'd come to help. With Calum, Torac, and Lachland, the search group numbered eleven.

According to Calum, the constable and another pair were riding through the forest toward the village looking for signs.

They divided into three groups, one going north to search, one south, and one east, since the constable and his group went west.

Torac, Lachland, and two men were to travel south. It would give him an opportunity to stop at the camp and see if the young man had seen or heard anything.

It was a torturous day. The warriors questioned every person they came across and no one seemed to have seen or heard anything of interest.

"What do ye think happened?" Lachland asked, his gaze scrutinizing. "Did she do something that could have caused it?"

Torac nodded. "I believe the man Tom is involved. He knows I killed his brother, and that Leana is important to me.

He is retaliating."

"Eli went to his home first," Calum stated. "It was the first place he went as he suspected the same. Tom was not there, nor has he returned."

"Is there a place he would go?" Torac asked the farmer who shook his head.

"I would nae know."

They finally returned to the camp to sleep. Despite being torn apart by worry, Torac fell into a deep slumber. His body overly tired from the continuous riding.

IT WAS USELESS to struggle against the bindings. Her wrists were raw from it and the pain unbearable. Leana had managed to push the cloth around her mouth away, but she kept quiet, not wishing the sleeping men to wake.

Their snores permeated the darkness as Leana tried to see what she could and get her bearings as to where they were.

They'd ridden for most of the night and the next day, but she'd been unable to see as they'd blindfolded her. Panicked as most of her face had been covered and struggling to breathe, she'd kept still. Terrified of what would happen.

As of yet, she'd not been able to identify who took her. It was two, perhaps three men, she'd been unable to tell. But none of them had sounded familiar when they'd spoken in short one- or two-word spurts at each other.

This was the first opportunity she'd had to attempt to escape.

It took a few tries and having to bite her lip against the

pain it caused, but she managed to bend at the waist, lift her legs up and untie her ankles.

Moving inch by inch, she slowly stood and then tiptoed toward a window. It was no use to go to the door as one of her captors slept in front of it.

With her hands still bound it would be difficult to open the window and climb through, but she had to try.

By the time she'd managed to open the shutters, just a bit at a time, tears and perspiration trickled down her face. Next, she pushed up onto a rickety chair and managed to climb onto the windowsill.

It was too dark to gauge how far to the ground, but she didn't think twice and leaped.

Pain stunned Leana and it took all her willpower not to cry out pain had traveled down her leg and a hot searing throbbing had begun.

Gasping to keep from making any sounds, Leana managed to sit up. Would it be possible to stand?

The need to escape gave her strength to stand and she hobbled forward, though running was impossible as her leg protested each move.

"No," she whispered. "Oh, God," she whimpered at the pain of each step. Somehow she managed to go a few minutes longer before having to lean on a tree to rest her leg.

When a tear trickled into her mouth, she wiped it away on her shoulder. It did little good to cry.

Determined to go further, she took several steps before stumbling to the ground. This time, she knew it would be harder to get up.

"There ye are wench." The voice sent shivers of terror

through her as she rolled to her back and saw Tom holding a torch. "I see ye require rescue."

A second man approached grabbed her by the arm and yanked her to stand. Leana cried out in pain and would have collapsed onto the ground if not for him holding her.

"She's injured her leg," the man said without emotion as if speaking of a horse. "What now?"

They sized her up for a long moment. The man lifted her and began walking back to the shack.

Once inside, he deposited her on the cot. Leana swallowed a cry of pain. "Can ye untie my hands, I beg of ye. I can nae feel them."

A man she didn't recognized came near and took a blade out and cut the bindings. "Only for a bit, I will have to tie ye to something to keep ye still."

Her left side continued to protest, but Leana could tell her leg wasn't broken as she could move it. The hip was injured, but she hoped it would be well enough by morning so she could try to escape again.

SHE WOKE TO the sounds of men talking outside. Unable to sit up since they'd bound strips of dirty cloth around her, pinning her arms to her sides.

"We can nae get coin for an injured woman," a man said. "Best to leave her and be done with it."

Tom replied, "Do what ye wish. I have no need of her. I paid ye to get her off the isle."

Leana was not surprised he'd orchestrated the entire thing.

There was a beat of silence. Finally, the same man replied, "Aye, fine."

"Have to return home. They will be looking for her," Tom said and moments later, she heard a horse galloping away.

If the man who remained decided to kill her, there was little she could do to defend herself. Here she lay trussed like a boar about to be roasted and all she could think of was that she was glad to have been with Torac and experienced making love. Her father would be heartbroken, how she wished it was possible to spare him the pain of it.

"I can nae do anything for ye." The man's voice startled her, and she looked up at him with round eyes. "But I can nae sell ye." He shrugged as he settled onto the same chair she'd used in her failed escape.

He lifted a wineskin to his lips. Then seeming to think about something neared Leana and poured the sour liquid down her throat. "Keep ye a bit uncaring."

She sputtered and coughed. He took advantage and poured more. It was whiskey as far as she could tell. The liquid burned a trail down her throat.

"No more," she said between coughs, but he pinched her nose shut and continued to pour the fiery liquid until it was all gone.

Her stomach protested and Leana swallowed to keep from getting sick. "What are ye planning to do?"

"I am going to leave ye be." He stood and grabbed a strip of cloth, then he wrapped it around the bottom of her face several times. "Ye will nae live long." His yellowed eyes met hers for a moment and then he walked out.

Had he given her poison? Leana rubbed her face against her shoulder in an attempt to remove the gag, but nothing worked. Her head was swimming and she managed to turn to her side.

When Leana woke, her head was pounding, and her stomach was in knots. It wouldn't do to get sick as she was still gagged. Rubbing her face against the wall, after managing to sit, she was finally able to lower the gag enough to take in a lungful of air. The one-room shack was dingy, the dirt floors as uninviting as the cracked door and putrid cot she lay on.

Hard as she tried, it proved impossible to get out of the bindings. With her arms pinned to her sides, her reach was quite limited. Frustrated, she lowered her bound feet to the floor and tried to figure out how to gain momentum to stand. The cot was low to the ground. It was possible to drop to the floor and perhaps crawl to the door.

Outside the wind blew, the chilly air falling over her as the dirty blanket the man had placed over her fell away.

She was not going to lie there and wait for death. As horrible as she felt, the resolve to survive was greater.

"Help me! Is anyone there?" she screamed loudly, the sound of her raspy voice taken by the outdoor louder ones of birdsong and wind.

Scanning the interior of the shack, she noted that there were several jagged edges to the door that hung lopsided. Hope rose and she rolled onto the floor. Each time she rolled again, her head and stomach protested, not to mention her throbbing leg. But she continued progressing slowly until she reached the door.

CHAPTER FIFTEEN

AFTER SEVERAL POUNDS on the door, did finally an older woman open it and stared at Torac and his companions.

"Go away. I told ye, Tom is not here." Her narrowed eyes took him in. "Ye are the one. Ye killed my lad."

The door opened wider, and Willa appeared. Unlike her mother, she did not appear as hostile. "Ye should leave. We can nae tell ye anything. Tom was here, but he went hunting."

"Hunting?" Torac repeated. The last time they'd stopped by Willa had sworn Tom had just left to go fishing.

"Aye." Willa's gaze moved down his body. "Leana is not worth all this trouble. She's a daft cow."

Not wishing to waste more time Torac turned away and walked to his mount. He looked at Lachland. "They may not know where he is."

"I agree," Lachland said. "It could be someone else was walking past and happened upon her."

"I have thought of that," Torac said. "But that Tom is also gone makes me suspicious."

Lachland looked to the cottage they'd just left. "He may be in there hiding from us."

Two days had passed, and they were no closer to finding Leana. There were other matters that had to be dealt with, like the attackers who'd burned down the farms and maimed

Balgair. If he were not personally involved with Leana, he'd have left the search to the villagers and concentrated equally on the other issues.

THEY RETURNED TO the camp to find Erik and several men meandering about. Erik neared. "What happens?"

He relayed the news about Leana. "Why are ye back?"

"More men arrived to help. Struan remained there, but the rest of us decided to return."

"I could use yer help," Torac said waiting for Erik to remind me of their more pressing duties.

Instead, the man met his gaze. "Let us go. In my estimation, if I were to hide a lass, I'd take her to the shore."

"The shore?" Torac asked.

"Aye. Take her to a bìrlinn and off the isle. If Tom is not at his home, he may be trying to sell her."

At the idea of what could be happening to Leana, his gut clenched. "To the east or west?"

Erik looked to the sky as if for answers. "Easier and less chance of being seen to the northwest."

It had not occurred to Torac to go to the northwestern shore. Just past Aldness, there was a busy area where ships docked that came from the northern isles. It was Stuart Ross' lands and very well watched.

At the same time, it was a busy village with different people about regularly. No one would think twice at seeing a man appear with a cart.

Despite being late and tired, Torac demanded they leave at once. The sooner they arrived the better, even though Leana was probably gone by now.

Erik agreed to go, along with four warriors. Everyone mounted a rested horse and began the trek north.

IT WAS LATE the next day when they arrived at the fishing village. Despite having ridden at a fast pace, it was almost dark, which would make it difficult to see much. One of the men was dispatched to inform Stuart Ross, while the rest rode to where Dougal Ross, cousin of the laird, and his wife Bree lived in a house on the hill overlooking the picturesque fishing village.

Despite the late hour, the constable's house was bustling with activity. Older boys opened the gates and took the horses' reins as they dismounted.

"We'll get them fed and in the stable," one older boy called out as they led the horses away.

The front door opened, and Dougal waved them inside, where they were greeted with aromas of food and a crackling fire in the hearth. Inside the main room the younger children were being entertained by a pair of older girls who appeared to be telling them a story.

"How many bairns do ye have?" Erik asked looking around.

Dougal shook his head. "Bree and I took in several children orphaned by a storm that decimated the village a pair of years ago. Since then four others, who lost their parents, showed up on our doorstep." He looked around as if trying to assess who else he should account for.

"Oh, aye, and my wife's sister and her three bairns are

visiting."

Just then a pretty woman entered with a tray of cups. "Meat broth to warm ye," she said walking to Torac, Erik, and the other two warriors. "Sit and rest. There is naught can be done until sunrise."

Once they took the cups of the flavorful broth, each drank the hot liquid with greed. Erik looked to where the woman Bree had disappeared. "Ye seem to keep busy."

Dougal nodded. "Since we were first married, we have always had a house full of people. Seems we attract them."

He looked to Torac. "I am sure yer visit has a serious purpose." Dougal listened as Torac repeated what had occurred and nodded every so often. "I believe to have seen a man that matches yer description. Mainly because he is quite robust, and I felt badly for his mount."

Torac leaned forward in his seat. "Was he alone?"

"Aye, he headed out of town, south." Dougal scratched his beard. "Lore, come here a moment, lad."

An older lad neared. "Aye?"

"Remember that man we commented on earlier? The one who was fat. Did ye see him anywhere in the village before?" Dougal looked to Torac and Erik. "Lore goes about the village to help the fishermen."

The boy thought for a moment. "I saw him the other day. He purchased fish from Burns"

"Did ye see where he went?" Torac asked standing up and pacing.

The lad shook his head. "No, sorry. I did nae pay attention."

"There are many places to hide around here, unfortunately," Dougal said. "Many come and find shelter until the ships arrive."

"I saw a ship offshore," Erik said. "Have any left recently?"

"Nay," Dougal replied. "'Tis almost winter, soon there will not be any. This one has been here for three or four days. They will leave in a couple more."

"We will go there in the morning," Torac said.

It was barely light and Torac was already near the shore. A small boat made its way from the ship, barely visible in the morning mist. It seemed to take forever before the men pulled it ashore and jumped from it.

"Do ye have any women aboard the ship?" Torac asked approaching them. "Has anyone given ye a woman to take away?"

The men frowned and looked at him as if he was crazy. "Are ye daft?" One man asked, who looked as if he'd not bathed for years. "Nay. No women."

"I know sometimes people try to sell women."

A different man spit on the ground. "Bad luck to have a woman aboard. It is not allowed."

"Perhaps without ye knowing someone could sneak a woman aboard."

"The captain would have their hide," a third man replied. "Someone did approach me the first day we arrived. Said he has a pretty lass to sell, but she was lame."

"Did he say where he kept her?" Torac wanted to shake the man who seemed anxious to get on with whatever they had planned.

"Somewhere over there," the man pointed. "A shack. Said we could have her, but I never relayed the message to anyone.

Could be a trap."

The lad, Lore, motioned for them to follow. "I can show ye where some abandoned shacks are."

Following the shoreline they rounded the cove and went to a particularly desolate area. Through the foliage, a pair of small buildings were visible. Torac urged his mount closer and called out for Leana.

"Leana!" He jumped from the horse and ran to the first shack that looked about to collapse and pulled the lopsided door open. "Leana!"

The room was empty except for a cot against the wall and a flat wineskin. The calls of the others sounded past the thudding of his heart as he followed what looked to be a trail of someone being dragged.

Had she been killed and dragged out to be buried?

Racing in the direction of the drag marks, he came to a solid stop at seeing a bound body that lay at the foot from a tree. It proved impossible to move, his body frozen, his lungs protesting that he didn't breathe.

"What is it?" Lachland came up beside him and then went quiet at seeing the woman who lay so still.

Finally, Torac yanked himself out of the stupor and ran to her. Her face scratched and dirty, and her hair a tangled mess, he almost didn't recognize her. But it was Leana. Her eyes were closed, and she seemed not to be breathing.

With a shaky hand, he touched her throat and took in a lungful of air at finding a slight pulse.

"She's alive," he called out to the others who'd now circled him. At once someone cut her bindings and someone else took off his tartan and wrapped it around her.

Lifting her up into his arms Torac headed toward his horse, but Lachland stopped him. "It is best ye take her into the shack than to chance a bumpy ride. I will build a fire to warm her up."

The young warrior was right. Leana was barely alive. It was possible she'd not survive a ride at the moment.

A warrior galloped away to inform the others that the lass had been found. Another rode to the village to fetch a healer.

Lachland remained to help Torac. He dragged the cot closer to the hearth as the fire began to gain strength.

"Take my tartan and place it on there. I will lay her upon it," Torac instructed while still holding Leana. Once it was completed, he carefully lowered her to the cot.

She was so cold to the touch, but her breathing soon became deeper and her pulse stronger. While she lay beside the fire, Torac fetched water in a small, cracked pot and after tearing a piece from his tunic, he cleaned her face.

Her wrists were raw from where she'd struggled against the restraints, but there was little he could do, but wash them.

The healer and Dougal arrived. He'd brought lanterns, bedding, clothes, and even a basket of food.

Soon the room was alight with the lanterns, and the healer inspected and dressed Leana's wrists.

"Wake up lass," Torac spoke into her ear. "Ye are safe now."

"Is she going to wake?" he asked the healer.

"When a person is exposed to the cold for a long time, it seems as if they go into a deep sleep. It is hard to bring them around, but I feel she will waken soon." The healer touched Leana's face. "She is warm. Give her time."

They spent the rest of the night taking turns watching over Leana, who continued to sleep. When the sun rose, she was still unresponsive.

"Leana. I am here," Torac said to her. "Wake up. Yer father will arrive and will need to see that ye are well."

Her eyelashes fluttered and his heartbeat quickened. She heard him.

He must have fallen asleep because a soft sound startled him awake.

"Torac?" The soft sound of Leana's voice startled him. "Where are we?"

He met her dazed eyes. "I found ye near here and brought ye inside to warm ye up. Graeme and two others are here."

She shivered. "I thought to die would have been better than lying outside in the cold. It was horrible." Tears trickled sideways down her cheeks and plopped onto the bedding. "I cannot believe ye found me."

"Do not cry. Ye are safe now. I promise." He pressed a kiss to her temple.

She clung to him as if her life depended on it, the solid feel of him bringing her safety. He gladly allowed her jagged nails to cut into his skin, the feeling that she was alive erasing any pain.

Finally, after some coaxing, she loosened her grip on him and the healer neared to check her again.

As much as Torac wanted to, he didn't ask what exactly had been done to her while she'd been held captive, it wasn't the time.

The urge to mount and hunt Tom Smith down was overwhelming to the point, Torac had to go outside to pace.

Upon the healer finishing, he would take Leana to Dougal's house to recover.

WHEN TORAC ENTERED the room, he was surprised to see how well Leana looked. Just a day of rest had done wonders. She met his gaze and immediately he knew something was wrong.

"How fare ye?" he asked tentatively. "Ye look well."

Her gaze fell to her clutched hands. "I am well. I owe ye my life."

"Do not say it. I would have—"

"No, ye would not have gone to such trouble over anyone else. I know ye left yer other duties to search for me."

"When ye are ready, I can take ye back home. I am sure yer father is anxious to see ye." He didn't move closer, it was obvious she was tense. "Is something wrong?"

Leana let out a long breath. "No. Nothing. I do ask that when ye take me home. Ye leave and not return."

"What are ye saying?" Torac neared and she shook her head. He persisted. "Not return to see ye?"

"Aye. I think it is best. All of this. Much of this could have been avoided if ye would have said something." Leana turned away. "Ye did nae say anything."

"It was just recently that I realized who he was. I did not know at first that Gawyn was the man who I killed while battling. It was when ye told me about the burn scar."

Leana wasn't listening. After going through so much, it was not the time to try to convince her that if anyone was to blame, it was Tom for allowing everyone to continue to blame her for Gawyn's disappearance.

"Very well. I will see about yer return." Torac studied her for a moment longer but when she refused to meet his gaze, he left.

CHAPTER SIXTEEN

FROM THE HILLTOP Torac could see Welland to the right, and a bit of the seashore straight ahead. The wind whipped around him. Its icy fingers doing their best to get through any gaps in his clothing.

"Seems a waste. No one in their right mind is out and about," Lachland grumbled.

"We have a duty to perform. But aye, I agree with ye," Torac replied. What he left unsaid was that he'd ride through hell itself to find Tom Smith. The bastard had to be somewhere. Hiding like the coward he was, he was also greedy and stupid. Sooner or later, Tom would surface, and he'd be there to make him pay for what he did to Leana.

He looked in the direction of the MacKern farm and grunted. The lass was stubborn but so was he. After a sennight or so, he would go see about her and begin his quest to regain her trust. Torac let out a breath. "Let us ride to Welland and seek something to eat."

They descended the hill, and he leaned over to run his hand down the horse's neck. "I will ensure ye have a warm stable for a few hours."

Lachland held up a hand and then motioned to a cusp of trees. "Someone is watching us."

"Could just be a curious hunter," Torac replied annoyed

that whoever it was could delay their arrival to the village.

"I will get a closer look." Lachland urged his mount toward the trees and Torac followed.

A man and woman with two young children cowered at seeing them. The man stood in front of his family. "We mean no harm. Just looking out for my family."

"Why are ye out here?" Torac asked. "Too cold for the bairns."

The man looked over his shoulder at the trio, who were huddled under furs, a small fire before them. They'd made a makeshift shelter from branches. By the pot and baskets, they'd been living there.

"The farmer who I worked for sent us away. We have nowhere to go until I find work," the man said. He stood proud despite his sad story and Torac admired him for it.

"Do ye have a horse?" Lachland said looking toward a wagon.

"We did," the man said, then looked down. "I had to sell him."

BY THE TIME they arrived at Welland, with the man's family in tow, Torac was hungry, cold, and exhausted. They'd hitched the wagon to Lachland's horse, as Torac's refused such indignity and brought the family to Welland.

Upon arriving, Torac sought out the constable.

"I do not recognize them," Athol said. "I am sure we can find them somewhere warm. Hamish died a few days back and his cottage is empty."

The constable sent for a pair of men, and they took the family away.

Torac and Lachland paid a lad to take their horses to the stables. Torac looked to the lad who held Brutus' reins. The warhorse seeming to know what was in store was calm. "Place the blanket over his back and ensure he has plenty of oats. Whatever most horses eat, he gets double."

The lad's eyes widened when Torac handed him a coin. "Plenty of water as well," the boy replied leading the horse away.

After a full meal and several tankards of ale, Torac fell asleep as soon as he climbed into bed.

Knocks woke him the next morning and he growled in annoyance. "What?" he called out, not in the mood to get out of bed.

The door opened and the constable peered in. "The man, who ye helped yesterday mentioned to me that he'd seen someone who sounds like Tom Smith. He said a bulky man came by their campsite and asked for food."

Torac was instantly awake and sat up. "Did he say anything else?"

"Said the man was injured, cradling his arm to his side. Headed toward Taernsby. It was a few days ago. He may have taken a birlinn and left the isle by now."

When the constable closed the door, Torac fell back onto the bed. His plan was to go see Leana that day. Would it be a better idea to go to Taernsby?

THE MACKERN FARM was as he remembered it. Welcoming even during the harsh weather. He'd told Lachland to remain in Welland. They'd stay another night before returning to the camp. The other three guards there could keep an eye out for any trouble in the lands between Welland and the sometimes-unfriendly village of Creag.

Once dismounted, he released Brutus to graze and went to the door. At his third knock, the door opened, and Eli stood looking up at him. "Come in out of the cold. Do ye wish to put yer horse in the stable?"

"I will nae be long," Torac replied. "I came to see how ye and Leana fare."

Leana was seated at the table. She looked up and upon seeing him, jumped to her feet and went to the kitchen and began moving things about, ignoring him.

Her father acted as if nothing was out of the ordinary. "Please sit. I have much to ask."

Leana looked over to him and upon meeting Torac's gaze, she turned back to whatever she was doing.

"Although we continue to do our best to find him, Tom continues to evade us," Torac said. "We do not know who the other man is and based on how Leana described him, it could be anyone."

The farmer turned to his daughter. "Warm up some of the delicious stew ye made." Then he looked at Torac with a soft smile. "Please stay and eat. I will see about yer horse." It was obvious the man gave time for Torac and Leana to have a private moment.

Leana scowled at the door when it closed behind her father.

"Have yer wrists healed?" Torac stood and walked to where she stirred a pot. "Let me see them."

"I am fine," Leana replied, not proffering her arm. "I have recovered."

Torac didn't try to touch her, instead he studied her right wrist. The scars were visible but seemed to have healed. "I hope the scars fade so they do not continue to remind ye of the horrible experience."

With extreme caution, Torac reached for her hand, stilling it from stirring. "Please talk to me. I miss ye."

Leana took a shaky breath. "I cannot stop thinking about it. If there was a way for me to see ye without feeling anger, but I am so mad at ye."

Finally, she looked up into his eyes. "Why did ye not say something?"

"Do ye think it would have stopped what happened?" Torac asked, still not releasing her hand. "I was about to tell ye just before Tom and Willa appeared. At first, I was not sure."

He let out an exasperated breath when she did not reply. "Leana, can ye try to forgive me? I wish to be with ye. To be part of yer life, both ye and yer father."

When she hung her head in defeat, he ached to pull her close. "Did they... did they take ye by force?"

Her head lifted and she shook it. "I am so thankful, they did not."

"They did hurt ye in other ways. I can see it in yer eyes and demeanor."

Pride swelled in him when she straightened and held her head up. "I do not wish to give them any more of me. I will ensure to be strong and continue on."

"What about me?" Torac asked, his gaze boring into hers. "Can ye make room for me in yer life?"

"Give me time," Leana said. "I care for ye, Torac. Yet, ye killed Gawyn. What will happen as we continue to live so close to his family? They will seek revenge. We will forever be looking over our shoulder."

It was then he understood why she hesitated. Leana wanted to protect him from whatever the Smith family could do to him.

"Can I hold ye?"

When she nodded Torac wrapped his arms around her body and held her close. "I miss ye."

Leana reached up and cupped his jaw. "I do as well."

After pressing a kiss to her forehead, he released her just as Eli walked in. He met Torac's gaze and gave a soft nod. "I am hungry, please join us for a meal."

They settled around the table. The aroma of the roasted meat and potatoes in a rich broth was as delicious as being able to remain in the same room with Leana.

Her father kept up the commentary, telling Torac about the livestock and his plans for the spring. The entire time, Leana remained silent.

"Would ye be opposed to moving?" Torac asked Eli who frowned.

The farmer looked past him out to the tree where his wife was buried. "I can never leave here."

"I am sorry," Torac quickly said. "I did not think."

Eli's lips curved. "If ye wish to take Leana away, I will not be opposed to it." He wagged a finger. "As long as it is not too far."

"I will never leave ye, Da," Leana said before meeting Torac's gaze. "I cannot go anywhere. Ye must understand.

That is why it is best ye not return."

The older man covered his daughter's hand with his. "I would not allow ye to sacrifice yer happiness for me."

Leana stood and walked away to the back room, closing the door firmly behind her.

"Stubborn that daughter of mine," Eli said and continued eating as if nothing occurred.

"She will never agree to leave."

The man shrugged. "I understand her hesitance for ye to come here. The Smiths are a vengeful lot. Over the years, they have been so unkind to Leana."

Torac pushed from the table. "Thank ye for the meal. I must be on my way. Tell Leana I will return in a few days."

The older man chuckled. "Good to see ye are as stubborn as she is."

UPON RETURNING TO Welland, Torac went in search of Lachland. The cold drizzle did little to dampen his spirits. Having seen Leana was just what he needed to continue on with the search for whoever took her.

Erik and several others were in the tavern. The laird had sent an additional five warriors to help with the attackers on the farms. Erik motioned him over.

"Another attack on a family. This time a small farm just north of here. There were four men, who headed in this direction." Erik's lips tightened. "We have to find them."

Another man at the table met Torac's gaze. "Although masked, the farmer thinks one of them was Tom Smith."

"They taunt us now," Torac replied. "Our inability to capture them is causing the people to doubt our abilities."

"Aye," Erik agreed and looked toward the doorway. "The rain will make it hard to follow their trail."

The attackers had taken what little money the farmer had. Fortunately because of the rain, the fire was not able to destroy most of the house. With the help of neighbors, they would be able to rebuild.

"They made a mistake this time," Lachland said. "They stole a horse with easily recognizable markings."

They motioned for a man at another table to come and repeat what he'd told the others before Torac arrived.

"Each leg is black from the knee down, like stockings. The rest of 'im is brown." The man shook his head. "A real shame as they cherished the beast since it was a foul."

"We will find them," Torac said, his face set. "If they headed toward here, let us search the woods between here and the Smith farm. He may be hoping to hide the horse in their stable."

The men exchanged looks. "It would be stupid of him to do that," Erik said. "I think we should search toward the shore. Perhaps one of them has a farm there."

"That is a good idea," Torac said. "Lachland, ye and Jamie go to the Smith's. The rest of us will go toward the shore."

Moments later they mounted and went their separate ways. The rain persisted, the drizzle as icy as the wind, pushing them to keep a quick pace.

"How are things with the MacKern lass?" Erik asked, his icy blue gaze meeting Torac's for a quick moment. "Are ye making plans with her?"

"She does nae want me to return. Is afraid the Smiths will find a way to kill me in retaliation for cutting down Gawyn."

Erik nodded. "Aye, and when ye kill Tom, they will have even more reason to wish ye dead."

"I am not sure what to do. They will never leave the farm. The mother is buried there. I may have to give up."

At his comment, Erik's eyes rounded. "Ye? Give up?"

"What can I do? It is not as if I can move the farm."

"True," Erik agreed. "But we can move the Smiths."

Torac laughed. "What burn their house down?"

"'Tis only the mother and daughter who will remain. They cannot tend the farm. Ye can purchase it. They will not know it is ye of course. It will make the MacKern farm larger, and they can live somewhere else."

"I never knew ye could be so scheming," Torac said, his heart lighter. Erik's idea had merit.

CHAPTER SEVENTEEN

"**M**EN APPROACH," BALGAIR said looking out the door of the cottage he and Swannoc had recently moved into. "Four, with a horse in tow."

His sword and battle ax remained accessible, next to the door. Although mostly recovered, he'd not tested his fighting skills as yet.

"We should bar the door," Swannoc said holding back the hounds, who'd also heard the approaching riders.

Balgair looked over his shoulder to the beauty. "I will nae cower in my own home." Straightening to his full height, he motioned for the dogs to remain and picked up his battle ax. "Say here."

Upon seeing him the men, who were in the process of dismounting froze. Obviously, they'd not expected a warrior. Balgair met each of their gazes. "Mount and keep going."

One of them, a particularly rotund man seemed exhausted. "We require some rest and food."

Balgair motioned to the wooded area to the right. "There is an abandoned cottage, not too far. Ye can rest there. I am sure ye can trap something to eat."

As they continued on, he studied the group and his heart quickened. Something about them seemed familiar. When realization struck, his heart began pounding harder. It was them. The ones responsible for his injuries. It had to be the ones who started the fires.

It seemed they'd not recognized him. Probably because he'd shaved his beard and Swannoc kept his hair trimmed.

Somehow he had to get word to Torac. But how? He could not very well leave Swannoc alone with them so near. There was the possibility they would return.

"What happens?" Swannoc said when he entered the house. "Ye look pale."

"I think it is them," Balgair replied. "The men who rob the families then burn down their homes."

Swannoc's eyes widened. "The ones who left ye for dead?"

"Aye."

"We must inform the guard." Swannoc rushed to where her cloak hung. "I will go. It is not so far."

"I cannot let ye go out in this weather." Balgair stood in the doorway to block her from nearing. "Nay."

In three long strides, Swannoc was nose-to-nose with him. "I traversed the lands alone long before I met ye and will do so whenever I decide to. Ye cannot stop me. The hounds will stay keep ye safe." She yanked the cloak over her shoulders, her direct gaze on him. "If they return. Kill them."

Speechless, Balgair stood silently while Swannoc strode out the front door.

Moments later, at the sound of a horse galloping away he went to the back window and watched as the hooded figure disappeared.

BY THAT AFTERNOON, Balgair had lost count of how many times he walked out to check for Swannoc's return. The rain stopped, but the wind continued its frigid swirls around man and beast.

The oblivious hounds thought it a delightful game to bound outdoors again and again. They raced in circles then returned to him with curious looks.

Once again he went out, this time the hounds raced away barking. Balgair gripped his battle ax as a group of riders came into view.

It was Ross guards, with them Swannoc. It was much too soon for her to have ridden to the camp and back, which meant they must have been headed there.

Torac and Erik both grinned at seeing him and raised hands in greeting.

Balgair couldn't help smiling in return. He'd truly missed his friends and the warrior life. Although living on the shore with Swannoc was much more enjoyable, by far.

There were another five warriors with them, he recognized them all from his duties as guard at the keep. All were battle-worthy men.

They dismounted and immediately Swannoc went to Balgair and wrapped her arms around his waist and pressed a kiss to his jaw. "Did ye fret over much?"

"I do not fret," Balgair said pulling her against him as he thanked God she was unharmed. "Go inside and warm up. Ye are frigid."

"Which way?" Erik said, by way of greeting.

Balgair was already mounting, his right side protesting only a bit. "I will take ye."

"Have ye been practicing with it?" Torac asked as they headed to the woods, his gaze on the battle ax.

"Nay. I use it mainly to intimidate."

"I would say it works," Erik said with a chuckle. "But ye should keep another weapon on hand."

"I have become adept with the bow and arrow." When Balgair pulled a broadsword and then a dagger, the men chuckled.

They quieted upon entering the woods, then a short while late they dismounted and tethered the horses so they could approach the cottage on foot.

The smell of a fire led them to the dilapidated shack. The idiot's horses blocked any view of Balgair and the others as they approached.

A FIRE BURNED in his stomach as Torac considered which man he would kill first. Tom was fast asleep, his head lolled to the side. The other three, he didn't recognize. One of them had to be who helped with Leana's abduction.

Upon Balgair's loud growl, they broke past the horses and onto the men who were startled awake, but unable to do more than stare up at them with looks of surprise.

"What do ye want?" Tom grumbled, sitting up clumsily, his arm in a sling. He glared at Torac. "We are not bothering a soul. Ye have no right to come upon us like this."

Torac who already loomed over the man, swung his sword, stopping a hair's breadth from the man's throat.

Tom instinctively shrank back. "Leave us be." He managed, his voice sounding strangled. When he went to push the sword away, Torac shook his head and Tom lowered his hand.

"Who helped ye take Leana?"

"I do nae know what ye speak of? I am injured, fell off my horse. How can I possibly take someone by force?" Tom said, his gaze sliding to the others as if in warning.

The tip of his sharp sword cut through the skin of Tom's neck and the man flinched, his eyes wide. "I had nothing to do with it." He pointed to a man who sat in front of Balgair. "It was him. All him."

"It was not," the other man retorted. "I never wanted to take the lass."

Torac pushed the sword just a bit deeper and Tom gasped. "Do not kill me. I will do anything…"

"We are taking ye all to Welland, where ye will admit to the constable that ye are the ones responsible for the attacks on the farmers, burning down houses, and stealing," Erik said his face taut.

One of the men tried to get away. Two guards grabbed him and tied him up. It was not much later that they escorted the four men away. Aware they would hang for their crimes, they kept asking to be released with promises to repay the farmers.

"How are ye going to repay the ones that died?" Torac asked one, who would not meet his gaze. "Or those ye injured and can no longer work?"

Balgair met his gaze, the old gleam seeming to have returned to the warrior's eyes. "They will repay by dying."

Upon returning to Balgair's house. The guards paused momentarily to say their farewells. Balgair entered the cottage to find Swannoc cooking.

She rushed to him, her gaze running over him, ensuring he

was not injured. "What happened?"

"There was no fight. Upon realizing they were outnumbered by battle-honed warriors, they did nae reach for any of their weapons."

"Good," Swannoc said and then gave him a knowing look. "Although I suspect ye are disappointed to have lost an opportunity to fight."

In truth, he'd hesitated before drawing his sword. The first thought that crossed his mind was that if he were killed, Swannoc would be left alone again.

"I do miss my old life sometimes. But I do not wish for it. The thought of leaving ye makes me realize I am where I should be."

His woman came closer and wrapped her arms around his waist. Swannoc placed her head on his shoulder and let out a long sigh. "I never thought to find love and happiness again. With ye, I have no need for anything else."

Balgair felt as if he'd won the greatest battle. No longer would he fight for more than to defend the love of his life.

"What are ye cooking?" he asked looking over her head to the pot over the fire.

"It will nae be ready for a while yet." Swannoc disengaged from him and went to the back door. "Go," she instructed the hounds who happily rushed outside.

She turned to Balgair. "Ye. Remove yer clothes, I must be sure there is naught a scratch anywhere on ye."

No longer embarrassed of his scarring, he quickly obliged. The way Swannoc's hungry gaze took him in left no doubt she found him desirable.

In response, his manhood swelled and hardened. She

walked to him and ran her hands down his chest. Balgair took her by the wrists and pulled them behind her back, then he took her mouth with his, tasting, devouring.

She struggled to be freed from his hold, barely, as Swannoc enjoyed his display of force. It was the only place she allowed him to overtake her—when making love.

"Balgair, take me," she hissed into his ear when he trailed his tongue down the side of her neck to her shoulder. Then holding both her hands with one of his, he pulled down the front of her dress, exposing two perfect breasts.

Taking each pink tip in turn, sucking it deeply into his mouth, he became harder at her moans of pleasure.

"Face the table," he commanded, and Swannoc pretended to resist. So he turned her toward it and bent her forward. He then lifted her skirts and threw them over her back to reveal her round bottom.

Holding her in place, he rubbed his hardness between them, each movement bringing him closer to completion. She was perfect for him, liking the way he teased her, brought her to the brink, and then stopped.

One hand on her left hip, he reached around Swannoc with the other and slid his fingers through her moist sex. Swannoc gasped and pushed back, she squirmed with each stroke over the sensitive bud at her very center.

"Balgair," she repeated. "I am about to lose control."

"Good," he whispered into her ear. Then bit down on her shoulder, not hard enough to hurt her, but enough to let her feel it through the haze of passion.

"Oh!" she cried out when he slipped a finger into her.

While sliding his sex between the orbs of her bottom, he

dipped his finger deeper, while teasing her nub with his thumb.

Swannoc began to tremble, a sign she was about to lose control and he stopped. Then took her by the shoulders and turned her to face him.

Trembling and barely able to stand, Swannoc tried to reach for him, but he kept her from it, instead pulling her against him and taking her mouth with his.

"I need to finish," she complained. "Please."

Taking pleasure from her need, he lifted her into his arms and walked to their large bed where he placed her.

She pulled her blouse off over her shoulders, and before she could finish removing her skirts, he impatiently climbed over her.

"I cannot wait." Balgair pushed her legs apart and drove into her until fully seated.

"Ahhh!" Swannoc cried out, her entire body shuddering. "More."

CHAPTER EIGHTEEN

L EANA HAD BEEN working in the garden all afternoon. She'd been digging up dead plants and turning the ground over to allow for nourishment needed for when it was time to plant again in the spring.

There were still a few potatoes and carrots on one side that were not as affected by the cold as they grew underground.

When Torac appeared, her heart skipped a beat. There was no denying how strong her feelings were. That he'd not given up on her and returned made her both happy and sad.

"I bring news," he said without preamble. "We've caught them, the men who've been burning the farms. Tom was with them."

Leana stood, wiping her hands clean with a cloth she kept in the harvesting basket. "Have they admitted to taking me?"

"Two blamed one another. Ye said one was Tom but did ye see the others. The constable would still like ye to testify against them."

Swallowing back anger, she met Torac's gaze. "What does it matter if they will not pay for what they did to me?"

"They will hang for their crimes. No one doubts they were who took ye with plans to sell ye."

Leana looked toward the neighboring farm. "Are they aware yet?"

"Someone is there now. I rode here with them, they are informing the mother and sister of what is about to happen. I am sure they will wish to see him... prior."

Despite everything, Leana could not help but feel badly for what Willa and her mother were going through at the moment. It was not their fault what Tom did.

"We should talk," Torac said moving closer. "About us."

"Why?" Leana asked. "I am not sure I can ask ye to leave yer life's work. I can nae leave my da. What can we do?" She ached to reach for him, to touch him, and feel his arms around her. Yet, she managed to keep from doing so.

Torac met her gaze for a long time. "Do ye nae wish to fight for me? To be with me?"

The question so simply put made Leana inhale sharply as she met his questioning gaze. "I do want to be with ye. More than anything."

"Then why do ye only see obstacles?"

"I suppose it is hard for me to expect good things." The honesty of her reply startled her. She'd not realized how true it was that she'd not expected anything more than a bad lot in life.

Torac looked to her house. "I spoke to yer da. He is not willing to leave here. But wishes ye to be happy. He says he has a good friend that could move in and live with him."

"A friend?" Leana looked to the cottage. "He has no such friend. If so, why do I not know?"

"It is a woman," Torac said with a soft curve to his lips. "Yer friend Beth's mother."

"Oh." Leana's mouth fell open. "I always wondered why he goes to visit there so often. I never realized..." She couldn't help but cover her mouth with both hands. "Da is in love?"

Torac shrugged. "Ye should ask him. I came to take ye to the village."

She and her father rode in the wagon to the village, with Torac as escort. The entire time, her father stole looks toward her.

"Are ye sure to want to do this? They will hang with or without yer testimony."

Leana shook her head. "I am not sure. So much violence. Although they do deserve to pay for what they've done, I cannot imagine what their families are going through at the moment."

"Ye are tender at heart," her father said with a soft smile. "Like yer mother. I am looking forward to seeing them hang. They did nae think twice about what they did to so many families. All for a bit of coin?"

Torac's silent presence made her feel better, safer. When had he become such a part of her that she could not imagine days without him.

"Da?" Leana began, unsure of how to approach the awkward topic. "What would ye do if I decide to go elsewhere to live?"

Her father gave her an amused look. "So ye and Torac have spoken." He glanced toward the warrior, who'd ridden ahead and was now out of earshot. "I wish for ye to be happy. Not to stay with me because ye feel ye should."

"I do not believe the tale ye told him about Beth's mother," Leana retorted. "I will nae leave ye alone. There are too many chores. I would miss ye. I will stay."

The village came into view and her stomach clenched.

There was no question how the day would end. Four men would die. There would be many testimonies and there was little Tom, or his companions could say that would sway against their punishment.

"I will wait a bit before going inside. Ye go on," Leana said, her voice trembling already. "I am not sure…"

"I am sure Torac will look after ye," her father said finding a place to pull the wagon forward so that he could tether the mare. The docile creature looked over at Leana when she climbed down as if sensing her nervousness.

Leana went to the horse and ran her hands down its nose. "Ye are a worrier like me," Leana told the animal, who nudged her hand seeking a treat. From the back of the wagon, she fetched two plump carrots that she fed the mare while waiting for Torac.

The warrior spoke to her father briefly and then came to where she stood.

"Are ye ready?"

DESPITE THE COLD weather, curious onlookers mingled near the main hall in the center of Welland. The men who'd been captured were being held inside and every seat was taken. Those who did not fit inside peered through windows.

Leana was glad for Torac escorting her inside as they had to push their way past people.

In the front of the room were the village council, as well as the clergy. And to the side were the four men with their hands and feet bound.

Tom looked to be in pain, his face pinched in a grimace. There were trails of tears on his dirty cheeks making him a pitiful caricature of the obnoxious man he usually was. Obviously he'd never expected things to come to this. To be tried and accused of murdering people.

They settled into a bench, next to where Beth and her husband sat. Her father joined them, squeezing in next to Beth's mother. Leana slid a glance to them, trying to decipher if it was true that her father and the woman had developed a deep friendship.

Daring to look over to where Willa consoled their mother, Leana met her gaze. Willa's gaze was blank, emotionless, almost as if she didn't recognize Leana. Of course, she was overcome with grief for her brother and mother.

"I do not wish to testify," Leana whispered to Torac. "Take me from here."

"Very well." Torac stood and once again helped part the sea of people as they went back out.

Once outside, Leana inhaled deeply. "It matters not what I say. They are to be punished with death. He lived there next to our farm all my life." Her voice shook with emotion.

He led her to the tavern, which was empty except for a man behind the counter.

"What happens?" he asked Torac.

"Farmers and families of those who were attacked are testifying against the four. Their fate is sealed."

"Aye, there will be a hanging before the end of the day," the man replied with resignation. "One of the men is my wife's brother. She is abed upstairs."

After sitting at a table, Torac brought ale and bread. "What about us?" he asked meeting her gaze. "Will ye come to be with me? Marry me, Leana."

It was what she wished for more than anything. "I must speak to Da. Make certain he is not making things up to keep me from staying."

"If he did. It is because yer happiness is important to him."

"I do not wish him to be alone. I cannot bear the thought of it."

"Once this is over, the trial and what comes after, we will discuss it. I warn ye," he said reaching for her hand and wrapping his fingers around it. "I will not give up until we are together."

Leana nodded. "I am thankful for yer steadfastness."

Time went fast, as she and Torac spent time in the tavern talking. She learned about his life as a youth, about a half-brother and his half-sister, who was married to one of the laird's brothers. Torac assured her, they would visit and that she would love his half-sister, Cait.

As the hours passed, the conversation between them didn't wane. They moved from the table to chairs before the cheery fire in the hearth, where they talked about their childhoods. Torac admitted to spending very little time with his mother, for which Leana admonished him.

Leana told him about life with Gawyn and how hard it had been for her to keep the truth of her relationship from her father.

A man burst through the front door. "They are about to hang. All four of them."

Torac stood and held out his hand. "Come. Ye should be present."

"I am not sure I can withstand it." Leana shuddered at the idea of watching someone's life end. But she also felt as if it would be the only way to get past what happened to her.

She took his hand and Torac's strength seeped from where they touched up her arm and into her chest.

"I am ready."

The four were to be hung at once. Four identical nooses thrown over a thick branch of a tree. The bound men were guided to the tree. Two of them fought against the guard, while one seemed on the brink of fainting. Tom cried like a baby, pleading for his life.

Leana couldn't help but think of the people who'd perished at the man's hands and yet here he was begging for leniency.

When the prisoners were pushed up to stand on wooden blocks, all seemed to fade. The sounds of people's murmurs, the icy wind, and the prepared speech spoken by the constable. The vicar stood before the crowed and prayed, his voice shaking with emotion. No one wanted this to happen and yet it would.

The constable called out each of the men's names, followed by a list of their crimes. After each list, he spoke the same punishment.

"Death, by hanging."

Some people cheered. Leana presumed them to be the families of those who died or lost everything. While the list of crimes were read out, some people called out additional things.

When Tom's name was announced, her father loudly called out, "He stole my daughter and left her for dead." It was the one crime that had not been mentioned inside, according to Beth.

The hanging was gruesome, Leana turned away, pushing her face into Torac's shoulder, unable to unsee it.

At a loud howl, Leana looked over. Tom's mother fell to the ground, Willa with her, both mourning the death of their son and brother. The families of one of the other men did the same. Some of the villagers took mercy on them and came to console them. Others looked over with disdain as if somehow it was their fault, what had happened.

"Come, let us go."

Leana looked to her father, who waved her away. Then he huddled with Beth's husband and several other men who spoke excitably.

"It is justice," Torac said leading her away. "What happened here will make men hesitate before committing crimes."

Leana could not fathom anyone wishing to do what the four had done, even without the possibility of paying with their lives. She let out a sigh. "I understand."

They walked toward the wagon. "I can wait for Father at the wagon, ye do not have to stay with me."

Torac pulled her against his side. Leana didn't protest the public display as most people were much too wrapped up at the hanging to pay them any mind. "I do have to return to the camp and see about things. I will return in a day or two. I expect a response to my question. That ye will be my wife."

He kissed her then. It was a deep passionate kiss, one that she never expected in public. Every part of her body immediately heated at the thought of how he felt devoid of clothes, his muscular body pressed over hers.

"Torac," Leana pushed him back. "People will see."

He glanced and then smiled down at her, a deep dimple forming on his right cheek. "I could nae go without leaving ye a reminder of how I feel."

Her insides melted, how she loved this man, how she desired him. Leana nodded her cheeks warming. "Go with care."

Before she could react, he pressed another kiss to her lips. "Talk with yer da."

CHAPTER NINETEEN

One Month Later

L EANA DIDN'T EXPECT for things to change so drastically. She walked through the small cottage, her entire body alight with the awareness that she and Torac would make a life there together.

It was a beautiful home, tucked at the end of a path with trees on both sides and a perfect little garden in the back. Although at the moment it was winter, she could picture the plants growing there.

It was a four-room cottage, with a kitchen and front room upon entry. To the right there were two separate bedchambers, each with a window to allow in air and light.

Her father ambled in with an armload of linens. "I did nae realize how many things ye had," he grumbled. "Two trips already, Leana."

A chuckle escaped at his complaints. She and Torac had compromised and agreed to live in a cottage that was not too far from the camp and the farm. Although it meant Torac would spend many nights at the camp, it would be fine.

From the cottage, she could take the cart and horse and be at the farm in an hour. She planned to go there every day to help with chores.

"I do not need yer help," her father repeated. He'd been

trying to dissuade her from coming since they'd made the decision on the cottage. "Ye can live closer to the camp. Yer husband will nae have to travel so far every day."

"'Tis not that far," Leana replied stubbornly. "'Tis less than it will take me to come see about ye."

"By the time ye hitch the wagon and manage to come, it will be longer than it will take me to do the chores meself."

Leana went to him and kissed his cheek. "Torac purchased this home for us. We both love it. Please be happy for me."

Her father looked around. "'Tis a fine home. Much larger than ours. He is providing for ye well."

With the money from the harvest, her father would be well set financially through the following year. Torac and several of the guards had come and completed repairs to the barn so that the animals would be warm for the winter.

Other than milking the cow, feeding the pigs and goats, most of the chores were few until spring.

"Is Beth's mother truly moving to live with ye?" Leana asked, still confused about how a relationship between her father and the sweet boisterous woman happened.

"Aye, 'tis more a companionship lass. We are friends. We talk about things we have in common, like losing the people we loved the most. She wishes for a space away from her son, so that he and Beth can enjoy more privacy, and I wish for someone to complain to now that ye will be here."

"It does make me feel better. She is quite demanding. Will have ye doing this and that."

Her father laughed. "I am used to that."

Leana couldn't help but laugh.

IT WAS LATE and Torac had yet to come home. Leana wondered how many evenings it would be like this that she would be alone, with only the company of a fire.

She walked outside and looked up at the darkening sky. Soon it would be night on her first full day at the cottage.

They'd spent the night there together the night before. It was the first time since their marriage that they'd actually been able to get away from everyone. Although they'd planned for an evening of lovemaking, both had fallen into an exhausted slumber after a quick interlude.

The wedding had been simple and celebrated at Beth's farm. They'd spent their first night and the following three days at her home.

At hearing whining, Leana followed the noise to a hollow in the woods, to find a dog heavy with pups.

"Oh, no. It is too cold for ye to have yer wee ones out here."

Leana ran inside and found some meat with which to coax the dog to a small shed behind the cottage. She then grabbed a blanket and hurried back out.

It did not take much coaxing, the poor dog was starving and gobbled up the meat, followed by a bowl of stew.

Once settled in the shed, which would provide shelter from the weather and warmth for the pups, Leana stacked wood from the pile around the outside walls to keep more of the wind out.

The dog slept soundly, grateful for the reprieve of trying to stay warm and find a place to have her litter.

Leana went into the shed and sat down next to it. The dog nuzzled her leg and let out a deep sigh. "Ye belonged to someone, I think," Leana said. "I am so sorry that ye cannot be with them."

She pulled her cloak around her shoulders and pulled her knees up. "I will sit with ye for a bit."

"LEANA!" TORAC'S FRANTIC call startled her, and Leana realized she'd fallen asleep.

"I am here," she called out just as he peered into the shed. He looked at her first and then to the dog who held up its head and gave a low growl.

"What are ye doing?" he said as she got to her feet and patted the dog's head in reassurance.

"I could nae let her have the litter out in the cold. The pups would die."

He glanced at the dog. "She looks like one of Auley's dogs. What is she doing so far from the camp?"

"Something must have scared her off then," Leana said. "I thought she acted as if used to human companionship."

Torac walked closer to the shed and pushed the door closed leaving it open just enough for the dog to be able to go in and out. "She should remain here for now. It will nae be much longer."

THEY WENT INSIDE where Leana realized that dinner was as cold as the entire cottage as the fire in the hearth had died down.

Torac went to the hearth and started the fire, adding a log to ensure it grew larger so it could warm up the space.

Leana stirred the pot and pushed it over the fire just enough so that it would warm up quickly.

Then she turned to find that Torac was gone.

"Torac?" She went to their bedchamber in search of her husband. He removed his cloak and went to the wash basin to rinse off the dirt of the day.

She leaned on the door frame to marvel at how this was to be her new life. To live with a man whose glance made butterflies appear in her stomach and chest tighten with joy.

"What are ye thinking?" Torac said nearing.

"I will tell ye later," Leana teased. "First we will eat."

SNUGGLED IN A pallet of blankets, against his shoulder, Leana could not fathom a more wonderful place to be. Tucked in his arms as they laid on the floor and watched the fire in the hearth enveloped in peaceful silence.

"I hope she will be well tonight. There may be many pups."

Torac chuckled. "Ye have already fed her twice and went to see about her many times. Sent me as well. The dog is fine. There may not be as many pups as ye think. Like ye, Auley overfeeds the dog."

He rolled to face her. "I missed ye today."

Leana leaned forward and pressed her lips to his. "I did ye as well."

There was urgency as his hands slid down to cup her bottom. Torac was already fully aroused, his hardness pushing against her.

"I want ye," Torac whispered into her ear then pressed kisses down the side of her face to her jaw and down to the base of her neck. "Ye are forever mine."

"I am," Leana replied, reaching up, to circle his neck with her arms. "All yers."

The throaty sound he made was as alluring as the vision of him as he lifted up and pulled his tunic off.

Leana shivered, but removed her nightdress, anxious to feel every inch of him against her skin.

When he lowered back down, she was glad for the warmth of his body. Torac held her breasts together and nuzzled between them, licking, sucking, and teasing each tip until heat traveled from her most private parts down her legs.

He was meticulous, ensuring not to spare an inch of each breast as he licked and suckled the sensitive skin.

Leana reached down, cupping his bottom and then sliding the palms of her hands up the wide expanse of his back.

When he descended down from her breasts, licking a trail down the center of her body, she let out a loud gasp.

Need surged and she took his hand guiding it between her legs, needing him to do more than lick and nibble.

Torac chuckled then took her hand and guided it to the now moist center. Leana wasn't sure what to expect, as she'd never dared to do it, to touch herself so freely. But when Torac lifted up, his hungry gaze where her hand was, she felt free to do so.

With her fingertips, Leana circled the nub between her legs, her eyes glued to Torac's face as he watched with so much intensity, it made her shudder almost immediately as her release came.

He then guided his hardness to enter her. First entering just a bit before withdrawing, each movement stoking the fire of a second release. Leana arched her back, her body alight with need.

Torac's arms circled her, lifting her onto his shaft and

guiding her down until she was filled.

It was different and wonderful, with him kneeling and her impaled on his cock as he lifted and lowered her in a steady pace. His muscles straining, adding to the allure.

"I have to finish," he gasped lowering Leana onto her back. Then he lifted her hips and proceeded to drive and thrust into her with so much force, she could barely keep up.

She flew and descended and still he continued the wonderful assault, his body glistening with perspiration, and every part of him taut as he held back, not wishing to come yet while his body screamed for it.

"Torac," Leana called out as she felt the edges of a third release. "Oh!"

"Not yet," Torac demanded pulling out and rolling her onto her stomach. "Lift up."

Her legs shook as she did as he asked only to give out when he drove into her again. This time he held her still as his movements continued. Faster and faster, harder and harder, each thrust sending sounds of their flesh slapping through the room, her cries of release mingling with his hoarse moans as he finally gave in.

His heated released spilled into her and Leana could only lay flat on her stomach trembling. Even the chilly air wasn't enough to persuade her to move.

"Leana. Did I hurt ye?" Torac rolled her over and peered down at her, his face etched with worry. "I am sorry."

She let out a soft chuckle. "I loved every moment."

Immediately he relaxed. "I do nae know why I was so rough. I will strive to be gentler."

"I wish for ye and I to allow our lovemaking to go where it

will. We cannot always control things."

He pulled her against him and then the blankets over them. At the same time, they kissed, wrapping their arms around each other's waists.

"I am glad ye are here," Leana said. Then she kissed him again. "So very glad."

TORAC'S BODY MOVED over her in a steady rhythm, each thrust slow and steady, his mouth next to hers, heated breaths brushing past her cheek to her ear. Leana held his hips, as she arched upward wanting him deeper.

A sweet heat enveloped her, and she gasped as ecstasy claimed her. Torac's moans an erotic sound that sent her to soar even higher as he too found his release.

"Good morrow. Did ye sleep well?" Torac's husky voice sounded in her ear.

"I did quite well," Leana replied pressing a kiss to his temple. "I could wake up like this every morn."

Torac withdrew from her and rolled to his back. "I will remain here for two more days. There is not much to be done and we have split the daily patrols into teams of four. I will go back to camp and remain for three days."

"Is this just for the winter?"

"Aye, once the weather warms, we will do more patrols and travel farther."

She lifted up to look out the windows. "It looks to be a sunny day."

"Good, there is much to do here," Torac said. "I must hunt for some meat and see about chopping more wood."

Leana watched contentedly as he dressed while listing all

the things he had to do. She smiled unable to keep from it. "Or we can go to Welland and get meat from the butcher. That way, ye can only chop wood and spend more time with yer wife."

He met her gaze. "We can."

"Get up wench." Torac yanked her from the warmth of the blankets and carried her totally naked to the table. "Feed me. I am hungry."

Leana squirmed. "What are ye doing?"

When he pushed her back and settled between her legs, she gasped. "Again?"

"Aye," Torac murmured, loosening his trews. "I am very hungry."

CHAPTER TWENTY

Two Months later

STRUAN GUIDED HIS horse alongside Torac's as they headed to the eastern shore. Once they arrived, they stopped atop a hill and scanned the shoreline.

"Wherever they are, they have a good hiding place," Torac said. "Or they have left."

"I grow weary of them attacking and getting away. They must have found a good hiding place. Once the birlinns arrive, I am going to find them," Struan replied.

He glanced at Torac who solemnly searched the area for any signs of people riding through.

"There," he said pointing to the side of a hill. "There is a pass there. I once found it, a long time ago."

They rode toward it. Struan looked over his shoulder and motioned for his men to follow. "How are ye finding marriage?"

Torac's lips curved. "I am enjoying it. Never considered how nice it is to have a home to come to and a willing wife to lay with."

Struan huffed. "'Tis only in the beginning. Soon it will not be so. Mark my word."

"Ye seem quite sure for a man never married," Torac replied, not seeming at all affected by Struan's prediction.

"I notice things. Have ye ever seen a married pair after a few years? They seem more annoyed with one another than not."

Torac thought to his parents who were embarrassingly demonstrative in front of him. "Some couples perhaps."

They grew silent as they progressed down the narrow path. "There," Struan said pointing to what looked to be an abandoned campsite. "Someone has been here."

"A large group," Torac said. "We have found where they hide. There are no boats."

Straight ahead, they could see a portion of the shoreline that would not be visible from back where they'd been on the hill.

"Next time they arrive we will be ready for them." Struan motioned to one of his men. "We will start posting men here regularly to keep watch for when they return."

The man nodded and rode away.

"Archers are a perfect choice for this assignment," Torac said. "I will return to camp and inform Erik of what happens. We have a pair of injured men after the last attack that will be glad to hear we have finally found how they can appear and disappear so easily."

STRUAN RODE INTO town with his men. They dispersed, some heading to the guardhouse, others to the tavern.

His stomach growled and he decided to follow the ones to the tavern. First he would stable his horse and pay for a room for the night as he was not in the mood to sleep with twenty other men, most of whom snored loudly.

As he walked from renting a room above the seamstresses' shop, he spotted Gavin, the man in charge of the guards.

"I heard the good news," the man said as they neared one another. "We will discuss patrols and such in the morrow."

"Good," Struan replied. "Right now I must eat. Are ye coming to the tavern?"

Gavin shook his head. "Nay, Alpena is preparing a meal, much better than what is offered there."

Struan looked over his shoulder to where he'd just left. "I am to remain in the place upstairs. Keep the noise down, I require sleep."

"We are but friends," Gavin said with a pointed look. "That is all."

"It matters not to me."

"Aye, I hear. Ye do not care much for women."

"They have their uses," Struan replied. "But aye, I prefer no feelings involved."

As they parted ways, Struan looked upwards, annoyed at Gavin's smug expression. What was it with men once they became enamored, they began pushing the idea on others? It was most aggravating.

"Sir?" a soft voice called, and he let out a sigh. Almost to the tavern and now someone bothered him.

"What is it?" His tone was sharp. A woman he'd never seen before stood next to a doorway. She was slender, with the darkest black hair and brightest blue eyes. She looked over her shoulder to the interior. "Do ye wish for company?"

Despite the offer, it was as if she was reluctant. Obviously, being forced by someone or by a situation. Although he did not care much for a woman's company, neither could he stand for them to be used in such a manner. It was different if they were willing, but not this, to be forced.

He walked toward her, and she seemed to shrink. "Who is

in there?"

"Just me...sir," she replied. Her almond-shaped eyes grew wide as if she were terrified. "Would ye like...some co-company?"

She'd never done it before, he was sure of it. "Where is yer family?"

The woman swallowed. "I am alone. The ship... offshore. I was on it."

A ship had capsized just recently, only a few people had perished as luckily it was close to the shore. Most of the people with the exception of a few had left.

"Why did ye stay here?"

"I was to meet my future husband here. He never came. Someone said he may have been hung."

Everyone knew about the four men who'd been hung. Struan wondered how the beautiful woman had come to meet one of them. "Yer family. Ye should return to them."

"They wanted to be rid of me," she replied bitterly. "I will not return."

"Ye cannot do this," Struan motioned to the tiny room with only a bed, a wash basin, and a chair. "It is not the way."

"How else can I eat," she replied weakly. "I have not eaten in two days."

"Get yer shawl," he ordered tersely. "I am headed to the tavern, ye can eat with me. After ye will speak to the seamstress, perhaps she can help ye find work."

"I have no coin to eat."

Struan let out an annoyed breath. "I will pay. I am very hungry and annoyed. Take this, put it away." He handed her a few coins. "Come."

Upon entering, everyone stopped mid-sentence and mid-bite to stare at him and the woman.

One of his men, Ian, was the first to recover. "Ye and a woman? That is new."

"Shut up," Struan said guiding the woman to a table, then lowered across from her.

The stunned silence continued until Struan stood and stared at them. "If one of ye touch a hair on... er, her head. Ye will answer to me." He sat down and motioned for one of the serving women.

"Two bowls of stew, filled to the rim, bread, butter, ale, and two tarts."

The woman hurried away after giving his companion a perplexed look. Obviously, no one knew the woman. He didn't plan to know her either.

"Thank ye," she whispered, her gaze downcast. "However, I am not sure I can accept the coins."

"Ye can work for them," he replied roughly, "I need tunics mended."

"I can do that. I like to sew," she replied, relaxing. "Thank ye."

"Stop thanking me," Struan said, then upon the serving woman returning, he moved to the table with his men leaving the woman to eat alone.

Ian frowned. "Who is she?"

"I have no idea," Struan said greedily eating. "Nor do I care to know."

"She is quite bonnie, is she not?" Ian persisted. "A beautiful lass."

"Ye heard me earlier," Struan said, unsure why he would stop Ian from seeking to know the woman. "She came from the ship that came ashore a fortnight ago."

"Ah, aye. She must have lost her kin."

"Hmm," Struan replied non-committedly.

When he finished eating and drank down his ale, he stood ready to go to bed and sleep. The table where the woman had been, was empty and cleaned. He'd not seen her leave.

He walked toward where he rented the room, which meant going past her house. In the distance, she hurried from the market with a bundle in her arms. Obviously, she'd purchased a few things with the money he'd given her.

If she didn't find a source of income, she would be forced to sell herself. A woman alone had few recourses.

It was not his problem to solve, Struan thought as he walked past the tiny one-room home and up the stairs to his room for the night. Although simple, the room he rented was a castle compared to her home.

Annoyed that she plagued his mind, Struan undressed and prepared for bed. There was much to do now that they could keep an eye out for the men who'd come and attacked.

Next time they came, the Clan Ross warriors would be prepared to fight.

Struan went to the window and looked. The entire village was dark, only a few lights shown from their windows.

His gaze went to the one-room home.

What was her name? He'd not asked.

Good, the less he knew about her the better.

Struan, a man who refuses love.
You will not want to put this book down.
Order your copy today!

A Note to Readers

Let's get to know one another,

Sign up for my newsletter and get a free Clan Ross story!

Newsletter Link: https://bit.ly/3vSEbYY

I sent out my newsletter monthly which includes book news, giveaways and sneak peeks!

ABOUT THE AUTHOR

Enticing. Engaging. Romance.

USA Today Bestselling Author Hildie McQueen writes strong brooding alphas who meet their match in feisty brave heroines. If you like stories with a mixture of passion, drama, and humor, you will love Hildie's storytelling where love wins every single time!

A fan of all things pink, Paris, and four-legged creatures, Hildie resides in eastern Georgia, USA, with her super-hero husband Kurt and three little yappy dogs.

Visit her website at www.hildiemcqueen.com.